Dark of the Night

John Winter

This edition published by Amazon 2017

Copyright © John Winter 2017

All rights reserved.

ISBN-13: 9781520333670

This collection of short stories is a work of fiction.
The names, characters, and incidents portrayed in them are work of the author's imagination. Any resemblance to actual persons, living or dead is entirely coincidental.

Except Joe, Joe's real.

Also, I might have based some characters on real people, but I won't tell them if you don't.

> To Claire
>
> Hope life is treating you well.
> Best wishes
> xxx
>
> John

DEDICATION

For Deb.

CONTENTS

Introduction	i
Divided	2
The Patron and the Artist	10
The Secret	27
The Watch	39
Sacrifice	50
Lucifer's Redemption	64
South Cove	81
A Long Way Home	89
The Other Side	100
The Fall	108
About the Author	117

INTRODUCTION

These stories were written over a number of years, some have their origins way back to 2007.
I hope that you enjoy this as much as I did writing them.

All the best

John Winter, Jan 2017.

DIVIDED

Last night the world rotated half as fast as it should. In the prolonged hours, he could hear sounds coming from the hole in his mind: conversations, soundscapes of memories – of things said, unsaid, and whispers of things to be.

He heard his dead wife's voice.

Haunted by the accident, hearing it, over and over. Her shouting, urging him onwards, and her last scream lost in a shriek of metal on metal.

Eight months later, he hasn't healed. If anything, the recollection has become imprinted onto his memory, just as the guilt, self-loathing, and pity have become his overcoat.

Mark is hung-over, again.

This was their place: a no-name restaurant that served cold beer and basket meals. It had chicken and fish on the menu, but both options tasted the same. Not that it mattered. Mary liked the ambience, and it suited their situation just fine; it allowed them to be out without costing the earth.

Mark closes his eyes and tilts backwards on his chair. Muted sounds from the bar filter through, distant.

Tonight the headache is worse. Solid. He worries the

pain, probing the boundary, as if it were a cavity in the roof of his mouth. There's something else as well; but it's like looking for a planet against a black sky. The hole in his mind has defined edges, snagging on ideas and recollections, inserting itself into scenes and past events with frightening clarity.

On his wedding day, he remembers speaking his vows, but instead of the Vicar he is talking to a swirling vortex. Everything else plays out the same, but the memory is corrupt.

It frightens him that his memories are slowly being erased, or altered.

He presses the palm of his hand into his forehead, tipping even further on the chair.

If the pain persists, he's going to have to do something about it.

Maybe.

Anything, but stop drinking.

A buzzing in his ears intensifies and he pushes his hand harder against his head. The pressure helps the pain.

His chair tips back. For a moment on two legs, then his balance goes. Mark falls.

He lands heavily, feet rapping the underside of the table with his toes, making the bottles jump.

His head strikes the stone floor and his teeth snap together. Stars flash in front of his eyes and he feels the cold, gritty, slab beneath his skull.

He lies there for a moment: No reason to get up, other than to continue drinking.

"Jesus, did you fall asleep?" Mary asks. "Are you day dreaming?"

A supernova goes off in his head and he falls inside out. Pressure, noise, and sound assault him making the act of standing upright as easy as running a marathon. Bile burns the back of his throat and his heart flops inside his chest. All the while his thoughts and ideas spiral into the remnants of a dying star.

Mary.

Headache gone, Mark brushes the spilt lager from his trousers and rights the chair. A few people have turned to see the commotion. He blinks, not knowing how he managed to end up falling off his chair, when he should be sitting opposite his wife.

She laughs.

Under the glaring eye of the barman, Mark rights the chair grinning from ear to ear.

He just can't help it.

Even the thought circling around, that he has forgotten something, something important, does not intrude on this moment.

"You're drunk." Mary says.

"Yeah. You're so beautiful." He pauses. Something important nagging him, but he can't place it.

"Ugh, come on. If we want to get the last train, we'd better make a move."

He glances at his watch, "Ten-forty."

Their closest train station was one of those little unmanned platforms, and the last train to the city left in five minutes. After that they'd have to find another way of getting home. Paying for a taxi defeated the purpose of their cheap night out. If they were going to spend that much money, then they might have well gone somewhere decent.

He reaches for his drink, but Mary knocks his hand away. "I think that you've had enough for tonight, besides there's something important that I need to tell you."

"What?"

"Later."

"No, tell me."

"You've been sitting in that chair most of the evening nearly asleep; it'll wait an hour. Let's go home. You can make me a cup of tea, and I'll tell you then."

That was that, there would be no getting it from her. Queen of the Schedule.

They run through the streets, shoulders touching when they lean into each other, enjoying the night air and freedom. Startling the sparse few pedestrians they breathlessly reach the platform just as the train doors start to close.

Mark is slightly faster, he manages to get between the doors, using his body to block it open.

The train is empty, he can see all the way to the driver's cabin.

The public address system clicks. Mark looks up, he thinks that a booming voice might tell him to step away from the door, but it's just static. Mary squeezes past him and they fall into the carriage together.

"Did not fancy walking home tonight." Mary says.

That idea, memory, shadow, whatever it is, is still circling, something he needs to tell her, but he can't remember. Instead, he looks at her, "I love you."

"Yeah, I know," she answers.

The train lurches forwards, stops, lurches again, before settling into smooth motion.

It carries on for another five minutes, two hundred yards short of the next station. It's an old part of the rail network, Victorian, width of a horse drawn carriage. Light from within the train illuminates the block stone walls of the tunnel on either side.

Mary frowns.

The speaker clicks again.

"What's going on?"

Mark shrugs. "Dunno."

He walks to the front of the carriage. The driver's door has a steel plate covering it with an eye hole. He peers through myopically, before knocking.

"Hello?"

A few seconds pass.

Mary stands by his shoulder.

"Hello!"

There is no sound from within.

"You think the driver's okay?"

He tries the handle, but it does not move.

"Give it five minutes; I'm sure we'll be on our way soon."

Time crawls on. Mark has the shadow looping through his mind. His foot taps a beat on the floor.

He marches to the door.

"What are you doing?"

He looks at his watch. "We need to get out of here. It's getting late." Public trains might not use the line after eleven, but it's a freight line.

Mark tries the handle again.

"Locked."

He uses the heel of his hand to bang on the door. "Hello! You okay in there?"

"What do we do?" Mary asks.

The speaker rasps white noise.

"Fuck!"

Mark kicks the door. Two, three solid blows. It doesn't even rattle in the frame. The shadow in his mind is starting to coalesce, thickening, but he can't worry about that now, even though it is skulking behind his eyes.

Then the bolt clicks.

Mark pulls and the door opens.

The driver is paper white, rigid in his chair.

Mary screams. Mark does too.

He checks the body. One eye dilated the other a pinpoint. He reaches across, touching the guard's neck. The man slides against the window, his whole body tilting like a board.

He pulls back. "No pulse."

"Who opened the door then?"

"Don't know, maybe it wasn't locked properly." He feels sick, could kicking have knocked the bolt loose?

Mary takes the guards arm.

"God, he's cold."

They peer through the front window. The tunnel continues beyond the circumference of the train's lights, and in the distance they can make out a yellow glow from the station ahead.

"It's not far, there should be a phone there, where we can dial for help."

Mark stiffens: Deja vu? The phantom behind his eyes watches.

"We need to move. The tunnel's only just wide enough for us. I don't like it."

Mark looks at the flashing dashboard. Nothing appears obvious to make the train move the last two hundred yards to the station. He tries pressing everything. Pulls all the levers and dials.

He takes the driver's door key and opens the exit.

It's a squeeze, he lowers Mary, then hangs onto handrail and lowers himself to the floor. His jacket scrapes against the tunnel wall behind him and snagging on the step in front.

A wave of nausea washes over him. There's a burning sensation, buried in his head.

Run.

It shouldn't be happening now.

He uses his smartphone to illuminate the sleepers, and stained granite chips so that they can see where they are going.

"Great." Mary complains.

Dust dislodged from the tunnel ceiling fall through the light beam.

"Vibration. Something's coming."

Mark knows what they have to do. There's no time to squeeze through behind the train, it would take them too long. The platform ahead is less than two hundred yards. He pulls Mary forward, getting behind her and ushering her along.

It's like the race they've run so many times before and a fraction of the distance. Mary sets the pace.

Legs pounding, he knows that they will make it. He can hear a rumbling noise now, the train getting closer.

He overtakes her, knowing that he can throw himself against the platform so that she can use him as a step to climb.

Only he can't hear her footfalls.

"Run!" she screams.

The sound of her voice came from within, from his own head, moments before Mary cries out.

He's been here before.

The light from his phone picks out her fallen form, scrabbling on the stones to get to her feet. Too slow.

Not only are the tracks vibrating, so too are the walls.

He runs back to her. A fire ignites in his head and his brain burns.

At her side, he shines the light around them. It's too far to get to the platform now, but he can see an inset cut into the wall.

Mark pulls Mary to her feet, it's small, too small for him to fit in, so he pushes her into the channel. Around them, the rumbling intensifies. He looks at her in the gap, and she motions for him to join her, but he knows that there's no room. If he does, the vacuum would take him, and her with him.

She has a chance like this.

Memories from a different time, a different universe re-imprint themselves.

Mark shakes his head.

He steps back.

The roar of the oncoming train is deafening. Bathed in white light, he smiles.

He tells her, "I have already seen a future without you."

Then he's gone.

What did he mean by that?

Mary wondered. She put her cordial drink down on the table, and wiped a line through the condensation.

The bar's busier, but she'd not noticed. Mark never found out that they were expecting. In saving her, he'd also saved their unborn son.

The barman saw her looking and waved, pointing to the door, where outside her taxi would be waiting.

She raised her glass to her lips, taking one last drink for Mark. This time there would be no breakneck race to the train station. She eases herself out of the chair, mindful of the extra weight.

She takes one last look around. Mary won't be here again, it was time to say goodbye to his ghost and look to the future.

THE PATRON AND THE ARTIST

Mum cried all the way to her sister's.

Dad's fault, again. I'd caught the tail end of their argument. The point when it became almost silent, other than the grunt of exertion and the sound of striking fists. The ups-and-downs of their relationship recorded in bruises upon our bodies.

I didn't want to go, but she did, and at twelve, I had no say.

I couldn't tell Mum that she'd chosen badly, and so too had her sister. For all I knew, that was the way it was with everybody. Between them, they had a lot in common. Both married to violent men, only her sister had endured it longer and had raised two equally violent sons.

They didn't hit as hard as Dad, not yet, but it wouldn't be long.

Dumped on the doorstep, and pointed in the direction of Old Kentish Town, I was told that my older delinquent cousins, Sebastian and Colin, were playing in the park.

To me, that was a good place to avoid.

I waited on the threshold, wanting to leave my

overnight bag in the house. As Mum was ushered inside beneath broken wings, the door closed on my face.

Taking my bag with me, I headed in the opposite direction.

I was looking through a newsagent's window when they found me. My heart skipped when I noticed two extra reflections next to my own.

Sebastian was holding a neon Nerf gun, wearing a red boxing helmet. I saw them, but pretended I hadn't. I'd only worn my gear to A&E. Dad used it to explain my injuries. So far, no one had noticed that the bloodied knuckles were on the wrong hands.

If I stared long enough into the glass, I thought they would go away.

A strong hand clamped on the back of my neck and my head accelerated towards the unyielding surface. It ricocheted off with a bang and I saw stars.

"Hey Steven, you dip-shit."

I twisted away from under his grasp, head throbbing, but I didn't want to give them the pleasure of knowing how much it hurt. I didn't even look at them. They were vampires. I'd learnt long ago that if I gave them nothing to feed on, their interest in me would wither and die. Gas Lighters, a term I'd picked up from one of Mum's self-help books.

I swallowed, and rubbed my head when I was far enough away not to be ridiculed.

I strode quickly, moving through side streets, keeping a mental bearing of how to get back to my Aunt's. But with each turn the surroundings looked less and less familiar. The last thing I wanted was to stop and ask directions. They kept pace, bouncing a tennis ball behind me. Sometimes it caught my heel, causing them both to shriek with laughter.

An hour, maybe longer, the torment continued. They'd

started to throw the ball against my back, adding to the bruises I already had there.

That's when I walked into a dead end.

Red brick walls of industrial units, decayed and derelict, blocked three sides. I stood at a blank wall, facing forwards, unsure what to do. The tennis ball thwacked above my head, returning to my tormentors, only to be hurled again, closer and closer.

I turned around.

The ball struck my shoulder and flew up and off at an angle, clattering against corrugated roof tiles.

Sebastian shook his head, "You gotta fetch that now."

"No." I replied.

"You were the last person to touch it." I hated him, hated him more than Dad. He said it as though we'd been in the middle of a game and it was an inconvenience to both of us. What did I care that it was lost?

The muscles twitched in Sebastian's jaw. The precursor to him losing it; just like our dads.

This could give them the excuse they were waiting for. Unless I fetched their stupid ball, it was only going to make things worse.

I looked at the wall, and for once, they looked in the same direction.

"You can use those broken bricks as handholds," Colin said. Colin was stupid.

I couldn't, they weren't deep enough to get my fingers into and they were clogged with salt. Instead, I used a metal waste bin to climb onto an adjacent wall and balanced across to the first roof. I had to be mindful not to get my feet caught on rusted razor wire.

Up here, I could see metal supports visible through holes in the asbestos panels. I looked at my cousins, then to the ball stuck in a gutter between two sloping units.

I inched forwards. Palms first, rolling my weight across my limbs.

"Come on!" Colin shouted.

I wondered if I could just stop. Crawl out of sight and stay there.

A vibration shuddered through my arm.

What the hell? The tennis ball popped free of the gutter, partly because the gutter was now falling inwards.

The roof tipped away from me. I rolled over, and my feet slammed through the brittle covering. Metal struts snapped, dropping me into the dark interior.

I kept my eyes shut against the pain. Nails pierced my back, three between my ribs and a couple along my spine. Agony flowed through me in cold waves. I couldn't move, not my hand to reach my phone, or even turn my head to the side.

I heard Sebastian and Colin talking, their voices drifting through the opening in the roof.

"Think he's dead?"

"Hopefully."

"Loser."

"Hey, dick head. If you are still alive, next time your mum runs here, tell her to put some money in your bag."

My belongings rained down through the gaping above. Followed by my now empty bag.

At this point, I would have welcomed death.

I lay waiting for something to happen: either enough blood to leak out of my body, or the creeping cold to overwhelm me. Neither of those things happened. I just went numb.

I tried to sit up, but all that happened was that I strained against the nails in my back. God it hurt.

I was stuck.

With nothing else to do, I watched the sky darken. Wondering how long it would take to die, wondering if I could will the onset of blood poisoning.

Above me, the stars twinkled indifferently.

I awoke to the sound of horse's hooves, scraping on stone outside the building.

Moonlight silvered the sky above and stars shone down casting faint shadows.

My view became blocked by the silhouette of a tall hat, one that would have made Dr. Seuss's cat jealous.

"Helloooo!" a voice called. "Anyone down there? Ah, oo - so there is."

A man, as ancient as Methuselah, dropped next to me, landing lightly. His red riding coat billowed from the fall, and he clutched a walking cane in one hand, to steady his balance.

"You poor fellow. You're pinned to a board dear boy, not quite the notice or poster I would expect." He walked around my prone form, "My, my, what is it that Maximillian can do?"

"My phone," I managed, my lips stiff and uncompliant. "Can you call for help? It's in my pocket."

"Yes! Max can help. Certainly!"

He reached in with the expertise of a pickpocket, and brought forth my Nokia.

"Ah. Alas, it appears to be broken."

He turned the handset in his hand, showing me the dead display.

The man sniffed loudly. "Well, maybe I could just give you a hand?"

"Don't!" I protested.

His cheeks hollowed as he readied himself to take the strain. With a hand, emaciated and withered, more similar to one of the desiccated mummies I'd seen in the natural history museum, he held mine. Still, there was strength in his grasp. With a sharp jerk, he pulled me from the nails like a cork popping from a champagne bottle.

Once upright, he brushed me down with his spidery fingers. His hand fleetingly caught where a nail had torn into my neck, and came away bloodied.

He rubbed his fingers together, distastefully peering at the dark stain.

"It is but a mere scratch."

I tried to reach around to feel the holes in my back, but he shook his head and slapped my hand away.

"How bad is it?"

"You're fine," he said, but his face said otherwise. He caught looking at him. "With all the blood, it looks worse than it is – you'll have to get a dab of ointment on your wounds, but for now, it's best that you don't touch."

I looked at the blank screen on my phone, no cracks in the glass, but no picture either.

The man shrugged out of his coat and wrapped it around my shoulders. As soon as the material touched my shoulders, I felt warmth start to return to my limbs. Along my spine the punctures started to tingle.

I tried to take it off, not wanting to get it bloody.

"No, keep it on. It will keep the chill at bay. Protect you."

"I just need to get…" what did I need? Had anyone noticed I was gone? Did Mum know? Did she even care?

"What do you need, dear boy?"

"I… I don't know."

He looked at my face, at the discoloured bruises left by my dad and the fresh bump from the window pane. He sighed, "Ah, the untold stories of the forgotten. All is not right in your world, is it my boy?"

I said nothing.

"You need to meet a friend of mine. A good friend. An artist. He can help."

"What do you mean help?"

"Trust me. Come, we can meet him. Put some ointment on those scratches and clean away some of the scars." He peered out from under the brim of his hat, "What's the matter, you afraid?"

I picked up my bag, surprised I could actually bend.

"I need to be going." I said.

"But where? What is so pressing that it couldn't wait for another hour? Have you been missed so much that they are out looking for you?"

I shook my head.

"What's your name?"

"Steven."

"I like that. A strong, solid name.

"Steven, I believe that I know someone who can help you, help you with this." He rubbed the flaking blood from his fingers. "What do you say?"

Where else had I to go? No one had come looking. Mum was too much in her own misery to notice I wasn't there. Maybe she thought I'd run away.

Maybe I should.

"Okay."

Max clapped his hands together, "Marvellous!"

"Where are we going?"

"I am taking you to The Theatre!" He removed a card from his top pocket and flicked it.

I tried to see, but he turned the card away from me. "My personal invitation. Do not be disturbed by the title, this is no Grand Guignol. The pleasures are far softer. Ahh," he said in reverie, as though savouring a fine wine. "While this is not a place for a fine young man as yourself, it is where the artist is." For an instant, his eyes shone like the setting sun through clouds.

Max was quite the eccentric, leading me down different streets looking for his theatre entrance. His theatre, as by this time I was sure it was a figment of his imagination. But what else was I to do?

I clutched my bag tighter, listening to the sound of the wind blow through broken windows and the overhead telephone cables rattling against their wooden masts.

"I'm sure it was around here somewhere," he said as he dipped to one side and produced a watch from his waistcoat. Max removed his hat and scratched thoughtfully. His silver hair was illuminated gold by the overhead streetlight, like the glass on the dial.

Snapping the watch shut, he set off again, cane rattling

against the tarmac every third step.

At last, he stopped before a recessed door. One I'm sure we passed several times, before knocking loudly.

"It's here," he announced.

A hatch slid open, spilling light and sound out into an otherwise empty street. Max produced the invitation and handed it through.

Silently the door opened and a suited doorman beckoned us both inside. Max smiled, tipping his hat.

A wave of warm air hit me, scents of cinnamon, tobacco, the tang of alcohol and something else. My skin prickled with energy.

"Your box is ready, with the usual arrangements, sir," the doorman bowed.

"I will be along in a moment." Max tipped his head toward me, while talking to the doorman. "While I'm sure he would want to see, the show is not for the innocent." Max leant against his cane, "I take it that Jacque is in his studio?"

"Indeed he is, sir."

"If you would be so good as to tell Isobella to warm my glass, I will be there before the cognac hits the crystal!" Max led me down a long corridor with multiple doors leading off. The closest was open and looked to be where the doorman had come from.

Max grinned. "This is the Theatre de la Nuit."

Gas lamps cast flickering pale light across dark oak panels. Off to each side were rooms, each with plaques on their doors. One or two had yellow stars above them.

"Backstage," Max explained, as we walked along. "There are three stages in total, but only ever one in use at any given time."

A door burst open behind me. I turned. Four women, wearing very little but feathered silk, raced into the corridor. Their skin, so pure and unmarred, contrasted against the black of their costumes. I stared. I'd never seen anyone as beautiful, not outside of a magazine. And the way they moved! Sensuous curves carried atop lithe long legs, all hip and sway. The lead girl stopped, and the other three continued into the back of her. I swallowed watching the Newton's cradle of breast and thigh.

They laughed, seeing me, mouth agape, before vanishing through a doorway.

I watched after them for a couple of seconds, hoping they would return.

"No point in loitering in the wings – Madame wouldn't like you spying on her girls. She can be very protective."

Max opened a door and headed up the stairs two at a time. "Jacque works from a different palette."

On the first floor, the windows overlooked a deserted street, misshapen buildings framed by the orange glow of distant streetlights.

Midway down the corridor, brilliant light shone from beneath a closed door. It looked like sunlight, not quite white, but warm and far brighter than the burning lamps that lined the walls.

Max rapped twice on the door.

The light from beneath vanished.

A voice called out, "*Oui? Qu'est-ce?*"

"It's me, Max."

"*Bon.*"

The light returned, then seconds later the door swung open.

Sunlight streamed through an open window that by all rights should have looked deeper into the building, or out onto a dark courtyard below.

Instead the scene was of rolling green hills which undulated away beneath a brilliant azure sky. Birds swooped and soared in the distance above silhouetted trees on the horizon.

The man standing before the view was unassuming, average, save for his beagle eyes and a brown beret. The whiskers down one side of his face were rainbow hued, colours that matched the tips of the digits of his hands.

The man raced to the window, and flipped it over. As it turned, sunlight arced across the room, illuminating a vast array of easels and canvases throughout. The new view was that of a night cityscape, resplendent sparkling distant lights.

"Jacque, I have to leave young Steven in your charge. He could very much do with seeing some of your marvellous paintings." Max dropped a hand onto my shoulder, "Something to bring cheer to his soul, chase his rainclouds away."

Max addressed me quietly, "I will be back within the hour. You will be safe here." Then he bowed deeply, "Farewell Jacque, until later Steven! The night calls!"

Then he was gone.

Jacque smiled, abashed, "Sorry I wasn't expecting visitors. Welcome to my studio."

At first I thought that the room was tiny, it wasn't. What I'd taken for a wall was a huge Victorian street scene, resplendent with wrought iron lampposts, claustrophobic buildings either side of a cobbled road. Before that there were four smaller canvases stood apart from the others, the largest covered by a sheet.

"Well, Master Steven, I am Jacque LeMarnier," he pushed his fingers through the start of a beard, smearing more pigments across his whiskered chin.

"Pleased to meet you, sir."

I shrugged out of Max's coat and gingerly felt where the nails had pierced my back, expecting it to be tender. It wasn't. Other than the hole in my clothes, I couldn't actually tell where the nails had gone in. He saw me twisting, shirt tenting wide at a tear, and I glanced down to see my own exposed chest, a mottled patchwork of bruises.

"And these were from tonight?" he pointed to an old one. Or rather, an area my dad labelled his fist magnet.

"It's nothing."

He took a deep breath, then let it out, taking the beret and wiping his forehead.

"Well," he smiled, "let me show you something." Standing he gestured to the scattered pictures around the room.

He motioned to the painting of a woman. I'd heard people use the expression that it was so realistic the eyes followed you. This was on the next level. I was looking at the bare back and shoulders of a woman, raven hair spilling down the side of her face. As I stepped closer to get a better look, she turned away from me, the strap of her dress falling from her shoulder.

"How did you do that?" No cables ran into the frame, I couldn't see power lights, it had to be video.

"This is Anna, my wife. At least how I remember her, she watches over me while I paint." He picked up a dark green drape and gently hung it over the frame. The woman in the picture turned and blew him a kiss before she disappeared from view. He touched his fingers to his lips, and pressed them against the folds of the sheet.

"How…?"

"Do you believe in magic?" he smiled. "Sometimes if you wish for something, if you wish for it with all your heart, you can capture it. Draw down your soul and work with it. With me, it's painting." He gestured around the room, "These are my wishes."

We walked around this displays and Jacque pointed to the night scene that I'd taken for a window, "Paris by night. You've already seen the other side. That was my father's farm in Montpelier. Good memories."

I must have pulled a face as his next question was, "Do you have good memories of home?"

I didn't like where this was going. "Some."

He nodded.

"What's that one over there?" I pointed to the largest covered painting.

"That will be a portrait of Madame Morte, the owner

of this place."

"Can I have a look?"

"*Non*. I've not started yet."

Jacque picked up a pallet knife and mixing plate. "I have to work on this street scene. You can help me." He worked quickly, sometimes turning the picture at the window to check the colours in daylight.

I mixed paints and cleaned brushes. I wondered if anyone had missed me yet. If Sebastian and Colin had told them what had happened.

While I worked, Jacque fixed a new canvas into a metal frame.

"Paint it with this, both sides. Do not touch surface." He passed me a bucket of black, pure darkness.

It looked evil.

"Is it poisonous?"

The tips of my fingers prickled, as they got closer to the surface.

"*Non, il va manger vos doigts!*"

"Sorry, what did you say?"

"Don't touch! It will… leave finger marks." I didn't think that was quite what he said.

I worked at his side, marvelling at the layers he built up. Outlines became defined, patches refined to recognisable shapes, only to be covered over by another layer. I watched him go over the same area with different solid hues, only for it to be smudged with a hand or fingers. Occasionally he would flick wine on the oils from his cup, or stop to take a long draught.

I felt my eyes close, arms aching from mixing pot after pot.

He smiled, "rest in the corner if you'd like? I've nearly finished this, and then I can start yours."

Jacque reached into the painting, turning a valve on the nearest lamppost. The flames in the picture died to glowing embers, lengthening the shadows about the room.

Eyes just about closed now, I could see him start to

work.

"What are you doing?" I asked, fighting sleep.

"Painting a picture for you."

I looked at the thick layer of blue that he had added in the centre.

"What is it?"

"This is a place where I used to go, my escape. It's a piece of sky."

Only half opening my eyes, I saw that a rejuvenated Max had returned. Where before he had been white haired and emaciated, now his face was free from wrinkles and a thick, black, mane curled from beneath his hat.

"Ah, there he is. Time to get you back where you can be found."

Jacque took the canvas, folded it and carefully fixed it into a wooden frame.

"Here," Jacque said, "is a means to escape whenever you want. Close your eyes, believe. *Croire.*" I heard the zip go on my bag. "Keep it safe."

I tried to stand, but couldn't.

"Sleep," Max instructed.

I don't remember exactly how I got back to the industrial unit, only fragments. I remember looking up at Max, or at least at this new version, and later Max brushing his hand along the rafter I'd been impaled upon as though smoothing a blanket. I heard nails bouncing off walls.

He lay me down, back where I fell.

My phone beeped. I heard the gentle tap of onscreen keys, then nothing.

Blackness.

When I opened my eyes, I thought I was looking up into one of Jacque's paintings: the picture of sky that he'd painted me. But he wouldn't have framed it with rusted iron or asbestos. And there wouldn't be two ugly familiar faces leering down at me.

They jerked out of the way.

I sat up and a rag fell off my chest, threadbare and decayed. Stray fibres clung to the board beneath me and where I lay was stained by blood or rust.

Dad burst through a door, falling over debris in the process, and Mum followed after, crying, sweeping me into her arms. Everything was all right. If only it could have stayed like that. To be held; to be loved.

Over a period of a month, the arguments started again. The shock of nearly losing me had only united them temporarily.

I closed my eyes and sat beneath the painting, shutting out the noise of their fighting. In my head, I sought imagined bird song, wanting, wishing, it to get louder.

"You can't leave me. You leave me and you're dead!" I heard him shout. "If I walk, I go out of that door and I'm not coming back!"

A slight breeze touched my face, followed by the scent of maple and blossom.

Solid footfalls sounded on the stairs, not dampened by the carpet.

The door to my bedroom crashed open. I jumped. Even though I expected him to come into my room, the ferocity frightened me.

He glared. His knuckles were cracked and swollen. I dropped my gaze, not wanting to meet his, in case he took that to be a sign of defiance.

His ragged breathing slowed, and I could hear him swallow, a dry, feverish click. Risking a glance, I saw that he was watching me.

Dad flipped a book from my shelf into the floor. I'd arranged them in order of importance.

Compensation gifts from Mum.

Works of James Herbert and Shaun Hutson hit the floor. A spider that had been hiding behind one managed to survive the drop and scuttled backwards to the base of the bookcase.

A rare Clive Barker followed, one of five hundred.

He was goading me, wanting me to react. Blood thudded through my ears and I could feel heat radiating from my face.

"Look-ie here. Isn't this one of your favourites?" A pristine Christine. I'd only read that one once, carefully bending the cover outwards to minimize the stress on the binding.

He folded it over in two, and then tore it apart. Both halves dropped onto the increasing pile.

His smile faded. He was no longer looking for a reaction for me, more intent on wholesale destruction of my prized possessions.

I looked at the painting, seeing the open blueness of the sky, wishing myself there, under the tranquillity, away from this, away from everything.

All I could hear was the sound of tearing paper, and somewhere in the background, Mum sobbing.

She wasn't dead. Hurt.

She'd given up. Given up on herself and given up on me.

"You little shit! Why don't you cry!?" he snarled.

I wondered what I'd done wrong. What I could have done to make him so angry?

There would be no reasoning, he wanted me to suffer, and that was all.

The spider made a tentative run, taking advantage of the break. It scuttled away from the bookcase, but bumped into Dad's shoe. It was a regular house spider, brown with tan stripes. I could see its black eyes reflecting light from the picture.

The picture - it was getting brighter.

My dad turned, I caught a whiff of his beery breath and the pungent tang of stale sweat, and his eyes fixed on the source of the light – seeing it for the first time.

He took a step forward. The spider, suddenly exposed,

ran towards the centre of the room, towards me.

Dad took the picture in his hands, turning it over, as confused as I had been.

I moved, launching myself at him, meaning to wrest it from his grasp.

I didn't even feel the blow that threw me against the shelves. The unit cracked back against the wall and I felt two ribs break. I landed heavily on the slew of papers, insides on fire.

Triumphantly, he held the painting above his head.

He drank in my sorrow. I was crying. Everything good in the world was gone.

He slammed the frame into the floor and it shattered. The canvas buckled and warped, slightly unfolding.

I could see the spider alter its direction, as it turned towards the fresh reservoir of darkness ahead.

Although clouded by tears, I saw. I saw the spider run into the blackness, its speck of a body spiralling away into a void.

I clutched my side. Hoping that Dad hadn't seen it, making as much noise as I could, anything to distract him from looking at the canvas.

I cried a world away.

It didn't take long for him to fall asleep, another couple of cans of beer in front of the television. I carefully picked up the painting, holding it by the bare material. On one side, the blue sky continued to shine, blowing air at my feet, the other was an inky mirror of blackness, sucking towards my legs as I carried it downstairs.

Fury made me silent.

I walked around the side of the chair, next to the table where he had emptied the contents of his pockets.

His eyes flicked open, and he looked at me. There was a complete lack of comprehension there, he saw me and smiled. I wonder if he saw his hate reflected, stored in a reservoir and now breaking through the dam.

I threw the black canvas over him. It wrapped around his head, sinking to his shoulders.

He stood. His heels kicked the chair and his hands waved through the space his head should have occupied.

A beheaded chicken, he thrashed, falling and slamming and crashing against the floor. Where the blackness touched the chair, it became worn and abraded.

I dropped behind the settee, listening to the banging and crashes getting louder. A lamp fell over. The television exploded, showering glass and sparks into the room.

Then it fell silent.

"Steven!" I heard Mum shout. "Steven!"

I looked over the edge to see the rest of my dad being pulling into the dark, toes drumming against the floorboards, until they too were gone.

Holding my side, I picked up his keys and wallet and dropped them in.

I carefully folded the canvas and slid it under the chair. I'd hide it in my bedroom later.

I hurried to the front door and threw it wide.

Mum came into the living room, standing like a spectre at the threshold, looking as though she didn't believe he was gone. Looking at me, then at the open doorway.

She didn't ask what happened. I didn't tell her.

She stood on the front step looking out into the night. I put my hand in hers and she said nothing.

The wind buffeted the door wanting to close it on my lie, the darkness outside bright in comparison to that of the underside of the painting.

We stood like this for an age, looking for a figure that I knew couldn't possibly be seen.

"That's it," she said, then more to herself, "he's gone."

Her fingers tightened around mine, then she closed the door.

THE SECRET

Six months after her death, Matthew slit his wrists. I held them, trying to staunch the blood and keep as much pressure on his wounds as possible. It covered me, soaking through my shirt, pouring down my legs in hot waves. He fell against me. Our foreheads touched as I struggled to keep him upright.

As we waited for the ambulance he cried, "Bethany's gone." Then quieter, "everyone's gone."

Two weeks later Matthew was discharged.
I look out for him.
I don't find it easy. I don't want to be around him, don't want to talk to him. On that score, that part's easy, Matthew is mute most of the time.

Tonight's different. Head down, still with that forlorn look of misery, he says, "I want to go out."

So, we head out. It's a relief. Far easier to distract him outside his house, than remain in the blackness that he's created within.

We walk into town, the silence as cold as the air around us.

At the traffic lights, I glance over: he's wearing an oversized body warmer, which belongs to his Mum. It's the only coat that he can slide over his swollen right hand. Something to do with severed tendons. The doctor said it could be months before he regains full control.

Bright lights from a knot of restaurants and bars glisten down the street. This is when I realise that heading into town might not be such a good idea.

"So, did you want something to eat?" I ask.

"No."

"Drink?"

"No."

"Cinema?"

"No."

That didn't really leave much. I lead the way down a side street looking for inspiration. It's hopeless, anything I suggest will be met with complete apathy.

I try so hard to be patient, but I'm pissed off.

So I stop. "Okay, so what do you want to do? You wanted to come out."

"This way," he mumbles, then turns sharply into an alleyway. At the other side, lights spill down the stone steps to the pavement in front of us. They come from the town hall.

"Here?" I question. I look around, trying to see what the pull might be to this dingy corner of the city. A tatty poster on a side door boasts a performance by Jillian Underwood. It's not clear who or what Jillian Underwood is or what she does - her name the biggest thing on the poster – so I guess she has a reputation, or an ego, neither of which appeal.

Matthew on the other hand is totally sold, "I wanna do this." Then sensing my reluctance adds, "Ten minutes, c'mon."

What harm can it do?

The dreadlocked space cadet serving behind the ticket booth gives me the impression that it's too much effort to sell tickets. "You know the show is nearly done. No refunds." He tuts when I don't have the exact change, then again when he passes the printed tickets through the window.

The house lights are low, auditorium silent. In the centre of a curtained stage sits a table.

As soon as I see the five people seated around it, hands linked like Christmas paper chains, my heart sinks. This is a séance. The usher herds us to our seats impatiently. I stumble headlong into the row first, focused on the cluster of empty spaces that are several pairs of feet and a mountain of handbags away.

Jillian Underwood looks like a dressmaker's pin; ash blond hair, cut into a polished bob that sits on guard upon her gaunt figure. Her voice, a total surprise, is more Sargent Major, than seaside sideshow. However, it's a pure cold reading, her answers mimetic and pliable dealt swiftly to the five people seated around her like a pack of cards. They lap it up, not minding that it took her five attempts to get from Mindy, through Mandy, Molly to Mark. My attention breaks when I realise Matthew is no longer behind me, and I hear his voice emanating from somewhere stage right.

"I want to talk to Bethany!" he pleads.

There is a heavy pause when the bracelets around Jillian's willowy wrists are all that can be heard. "Sorry, no," she says. "I cannot do that now."

"I have to talk to Bethany!" Matthew says.

There's movement from the side, three figures surge towards Matthew. I'm nearly out of the row when my foot snags a handbag. I fall onto an elderly gentleman, who shrieks and rolls me off his lap onto the floor.

Matthew, surrounded by three security guards, points at the stage, his injured arm stabbing the air. One of them claps a hand on his shoulder, and Matthew turns, hand still up. Completely by accident, he pokes the guy in the eye, who reels away.

The other two, retaliate. I see a blow land on Matthew's chin, rocking him back on his heels, arms out wide to stop himself from falling over. They grab him and carry him out of the building. He's out of sight before I can even get half-way to the stage.

Jillian asks for quiet; and the audience calms. She looks in my direction, even this far away I can feel her grey eyes boring into my head.

I find Matthew in the car park, scuffed and bruised. He's sitting on the floor, resting against a concrete bollard. I look at the torn sleeves on his shirt, expecting to see a growing blood stain seeping through. There's a scrape down his thigh, and his jeans have holes in both knees.

"You okay?"

"Where the fuck were you?" His hands are shaking, I can see that one end of a bandage has come undone. A safety pin dangles from a loose strip.

He meant to come here. Must have known about it for a while.

"Let's go," I say.

"I'm not going. I want to see Jillian. I want to talk to her."

"Come on. It's a load of shit. And you know it," I say.

"Anything is worth a try. I need to talk to her," Matthew hisses.

"Are you guys okay?" A man, in his early thirties, walks across the tarmac towards us.

"I think so," I say.

He looks back at the building. "Impressive huh? I was supposed to be here for a show, but I guess I'm kind of late." His voice wavers as he notices Matthew trying to pick at one of his stitches with his teeth. "Sure looks painful."

"Yeah, what would you know?" Matthew hisses.

"I - uh, have one just like it." With a nonchalant smile, he rolls up one sleeve. In the twilight, I can make out the criss-crossed scar tissue that runs the length of his forearm. "Did you see the show?"

"For about a minute." I say.

"Ah, so what did you think of Jillian."

"She's a bitch!" Matthew says.

"Yep, she is – what did she do to you?"

"Wouldn't let me talk to Bethany."

"I see... well don't be too harsh on her, would it help her cause if I were to say that she asked me to see if you were okay?"

I flush violently. "Sorry."

"I'm Joe." He holds out his hand, and I get another look at his healed injuries.

"Thomas."

He nods in Matthew's direction, but talks to me. "Let's get this fella home."

On the way, he asks about Bethany, so I tell him about the accident. That her walk to college had been cut short when a truck mounted the pavement and struck her.

He pauses, "You know that life and death aren't on opposite sides of the coin, right?"

I try to reason that one through, but I don't get it. I might as well be trying to work out how to smell blue, or group numbers by colour. Dead is dead, right?

Joe follows us inside. There's no one else home.

Matthew drops his coat on the floor, just inside the door and goes through into the living room. He lies on the settee, his face buried into the cushions.

"Make sure Matthew doesn't do anything stupid before I get back."

"You're coming back?" I ask.

"Yeah," he replies. He adjusts his collar, levels me with eyes alight with madness and adds "I'm off to fetch Bethany."

"What the Hell are you talking about?"

He grins, "Trust me," and opens the door to the cupboard under the stairs. He steps in and closes it.

"What the fuck?!" I reach the door, throwing it open so hard that the handle comes away in my hand.

I peer in, expecting to see Joe, but instead there's a heap of deck chairs, a vacuum, and a plastic set of drawers stuffed with tools.

Joe's vanished.

I quickly push the door closed, glance down the empty hallway. There's no way he could have got past me.

Prising the cupboard open, I tiptoe inside, or at least that's my intention, only I stub my toe on the drawers and set off an avalanche of spanners.

He's really gone. The gears in my head freewheel.

The sound of running water breaks my thoughts. Did Matthew shuffle past me a while ago? I was too busy trying to work out what had just happened, but then Joe's words came back to haunt me. At this moment, Matthew and stupid were one and the same.

I take the stairs so fast that my right leg thinks there's one more than there is and I stumble onto the landing.

At the same time, Matthew floats out of the bathroom.

I regain balance and he sees me looking at his wrists. The bandages are still there. In his functioning hand, he has a blister pack of pills.

I gesture towards it.

"Headache," he snarls.

"Give them here."

He throws them at my feet, so that I have to pick them up. Four blisters have already been popped.

"You taken any?" I accuse.

"Yeah," He folds his arms, glares, teeth clenching, then spits: "Two."

"So, what you doing with all these?" I hold the pack up.

"Taking them, every four fucking hours."

Reluctantly, I hand them back. There's probably not enough in there to make him constipated, let alone kill.

"Look," he sighs, "I'm not going to do anything."

"Yeah? That's what you said that last time. You know that guy who was here, Joe? He's gone!"

"So?"

"He vanished, stepped -"

"Good. I didn't like him," Matthew snaps.

We stand on the landing, gunslingers, waiting for the other to make the first move.

"You dick." he says and barges me out of the way.

I wait until he's past before I give the back of his head the finger.

"Yeah, love you too."

The outside of the house flares brightly beneath the window.

I flinch. That's where the security light is. Someone is in the back garden.

From where I stand, I pull back the blind on the landing and look down onto the path that runs along the house to the back door.

Joe is half way along the path. He has a body wrapped in a pale green sheet over his shoulders. As he walks, the sheet works its way loose, and I can make out long dark hair that trails down an arm.

Matthew hasn't seen this, he is already in his bedroom with the door closed.

I race downstairs to the kitchen, just as Joe enters.

"What the fuck!?"

He doesn't answer, instead he walks past. The hospital sheet hangs like a sail from a pale, bare foot.

"I need, maybe a minute, then you can come through," he says.

I ignore him, and tailgate. My eyes fix on the small white print with 'property of pathology,' that repeats itself over and over across the sheet.

"What the fuck!"

It's not Bethany, I don't know who it is. I do know where the hospital is, and that's miles from here.

A series of images run through my mind, as I try to rationalise how Joe could get a body all the way across town. He places the girl in a chair in the corner, propping it up with cushions as best he can, but she still slumps to one side.

He steps back as though arranging a giant bouquet of flowers making minor adjustments here and there.

I notice a growing bloodstain on the carpet near her foot.

My brain flips, and denies everything. I'm having a seizure.

"*Are you totally insane?!*" I manage.

"Last time I checked, yes." He puts another cushion behind the body. "Matthew wants to talk to Bethany, so get him. Quick. We don't have much time, the neighbour saw me walking past their front window. I'd say that we have about five minutes, tops, before the police start banging on that door." He motions to the trail of black congealed blood that leads through the house. "You need to get rid of that, now."

Joe positions her neck so that she's facing the door. Part of her hair sticks up on one side, matted together with dried blood and frozen in place. Her eyes, one completely opaque, the other black, stare through me.

None of this is real. It can't be. I pinch my bicep hard enough to dislodge a fingernail. It doesn't go away.

He stands, lifting the bottom of the curtain and lowering the lace over her head to create a veil.

"Why does it hurt, Joe?"

My blood freezes at the sound of her voice.

It sounds like Bethany.

"Why does it hurt so much?" she repeats, her voice low, broken.

He kneels next to the chair and takes her lifeless hand.

"The pain isn't your own; you're borrowing a body for a while. Sorry, it's the best I could do. When it starts to get bad, tell me."

"Okay," Bethany rasps.
"Who is... was she?" I say.
"Let's just say, a friend," Joe says.
"Thomas, are you there?"
"Holy shit!" Matthew says from the door.

Joe shakes his head, "You do not want to be caught like this." He ushers Matthew forward with one hand, and waves me out with the other.

"Bucket! Mop! Police!" Joe snaps.
"But!"

He grabs me and throws me out of the room.

There's a dead woman, talking in the other room, and somehow I drift on autopilot. The lights are on, but there is definitely no one home. I take a bucket from the cupboard, wondering if I step in and shut the door, if I would step into a different reality, but instead I get the detergent from under the sink, and do as I'm told. The running water blocks out most of the conversation in the other room. A chorus of 'why', precedes Matthew's inconsolable wails.

Joe's stands sentinel, stopping me from returning.

That's it. Over. Matthew bolts from the room, face slick with tears. His footfalls pound up the stairs, seconds later a door slams making the light fittings jump.

Joe ducks back into the room. I follow.

"Joe, you need to take me back," Bethany asks.

He draws her forwards, about to lift her.

"No, not yet. Where's Thomas?"

"I'm here," I say.

Joe lets her body fall back to the chair, the veil slides down over her face once more.

"Closer," she beckons.

My gaze lifts from the bare foot poking out from beneath the sheet, to her hand that lies on the armrest. Her eyes gleam from between the weave of the lace, glistening like polished nails.

"Thomas," she says. Her voice, quiet, fades.

I step forward. My head feels empty, other than my pulse, pounding fists against the inside of my skull. I can't breathe.

"Close your eyes. Remember me as I was."

I can't. I can't make the image of the dead girl go away! Then, something flips inside, and I do. I remember her, remember her before Matthew.

"What do you want?" I ask.

"I want you to know." Bethany says, "I lied."

The words have weight, pulling my mind downward. My legs tremble, and my stomach shrinks.

"About what?" I'm not sure that I really want the answer.

"It wouldn't have worked between us, so I finished with him. I killed his dream, so that he can move on," Bethany says.

The side of the chair presses against my leg and I overbalance. In the instance that I'm falling, my hand brushes against cotton, then the smooth cold skin of her arm. Her fingers latch over my hand.

"Matthew deserves a chance to go on. I love him, I do. He gains nothing by joining me."

I chew the inside of my cheek, as a distraction from the sensation on my arm, freezing, beneath her cold grasp. I wonder if she knew how I felt? That I wasn't here for Matthew, but for her.

"This is not life. What we could have had, that potential is lost. Where I am now, it's different. You've tried reasoning with him. Look where it got you. I can't do that. I'm not here anymore. If I tell him what he wants to hear, what happens when he needs to hear it again? It has to be this way, but, you need to know how I really feel. Only, that won't help him. Or you."

The bones in my hand crush together in her grip. At this point, she's the only thing stopping me from falling over.

"The truth doesn't matter now," she says, "only what he believes. If he thinks that you were in love with me, he'll use that against you, it will distract him long enough to go on living."

A low moan escapes her throat. I can feel Joe's presence behind me, ready.

"Can you pretend for me? Can you carry this in your heart?"

I want to tell her that it's true, that it wouldn't be a lie, but I can't. I can't find the words.

"Yes," I hear myself say.

"Thank you, Thomas. He'll be mad, hate you for it, feel betrayed, but I know him. He'll calm down. Maybe one day you can tell him the truth."

"That wouldn't be a good idea," I say. Not a good idea at all.

She holds me for a second longer, and then her hand gently slides back onto her lap.

Joe puts a hand on my shoulder.

"She has to go now."

I move away so that he can pick her up. He draws one of her arms up and pulls her into a fireman's lift. Her head lolls to one side as though it's on ball bearings, and fresh droplets of blood pat onto the carpet. Bethany has gone. All that remains is the shell of a dead girl.

I blink, my vision a kaleidoscope of tears.

"Salt. Mix into a paste, then dab the stain to lift it out. If you have time."

We don't. Joe sucks air through his teeth, as we both see the red and blue lights bouncing through gaps in the curtains across the ceiling.

"Good luck," he says.

Outside, I hear car doors pop open.

Joe walks into the hallway and disappears.

Shadows of police officers take up strategic positions either side of the window.

It will be moments before they come in.

I know that when they do, I'll tell them the truth. All of it.

And Matthew, I'll tell him.

Better to be hated for who I am, than continue living a lie.

THE WATCH

I stole a ghost.

I didn't know it at the time. I didn't even believe they existed.

It came with an old watch, and there was nothing about the antique timepiece that suggested it was haunted. The gold inlaid face and precise movement of the three hands spoke quality, as did its weight in my hand. I could tell it was expensive.

It was, but not financially.

My head spun. I had to think of a way that I could talk it up to Bosco, the owner and sole employee, of Bosco's Pawn Emporium. In the past, whenever I had anything like this, I wouldn't even get it beneath the iron grill that separated him from his customers without his eyes going all glassy. He'd squint at me through the corner of the metalwork as though looking through cross hairs. He knew the cost of things, and if I didn't have a good story, what I'd get for it would be less than I could sell it for scrap. He was a shark when it came to gold or silver. If the gears were jewelled, he'd know the value of each stone, then talk you down because they were from a flawed batch. If I could make him think that I knew more about it than he did, if I could find a hallmark or some other way to prove that it was genuine - then there was a chance that he wouldn't argue my cut away.

Where to begin?

You don't know me, but you at least know someone

like me.

I'm the person that you avoid sitting next to on the bus, or train; and with my dead-beat brother, Jason, we'd be rowdy drunks at the bar, scaring away the customers and intimidating the staff. Add Dave, who completes our trio, then we're trouble. Inconsiderate, unthinking, violent, hedonistic – basically, we're scum.

It's who I am: lazy, laced with obnoxious.

Have I always been like this? I guess so. Circumstance might have set me down in the neighbourhood, but my decisions determined the roads I walked.

It's a hell of a wake-up call. Least now I recognise my failings and have the chance to change.

Looking back, peer pressure played a big part of who I am; I was hiding in plain sight by victimising others to disguise my own weaknesses.

When I was a kid, an English teacher used to live in the same block as us. This was before I'd graduated into being a fully qualified drop out, and was merely a disappointment. He talked to me, perhaps he knew Jason and thought there was still a chance that I wouldn't turn out like my brother. He lent me a very old copy of Frankenstein and told me to read it, think about the monster, Frankenstein's creation. I was sure it was a message for me, some parallel that I could draw. Whatever it was, I never found it. I didn't finish. Jason made me give the book back one page at a time, through the teacher's letterbox, after wiping his arse with it.

What that taught me, was that if you piss off enough people, hate becomes natural.

I still think about that, even now, even with this ghost after me.

I ask you, what would you have done? What if your brother was the person that your mother warned you not to hang around with? No getting away from it, I am the product of those around me.

I have the watch. Not Jason. Not Bosco.

How did I come by it?

Bad luck? Yeah, but in some way. I invited it upon myself. Although unconnected, from the moment I pushed the first, stained, page through Thornton's door, which set me down a particular path. Do bad things to people and bad things get done unto you.

If it hadn't been this, then it would have been something else. In a way, this was my personal Jesus.

The three of us were heading back from Manchester to Leeds. We'd been down to give Dave's dealer a hard time, but ended up doing business with him instead. By the time we arrived at Piccadilly on our homeward leg, we were buzzing and looking for trouble.

I didn't know his name then, but Joe got on the train at the same time we did. Half an hour into the journey, Jason pointed at him and said that he'd not blinked since sitting down. Completely stoned. So we thought.

Yeah, what happened next doesn't paint me in a good light, but I'm being honest with you. That was me then, this is me now. I'm a changed man, I am. I'm sorry. So this is like describing the actions of someone else.

I'm not like that now. Okay?

We waited a bit, biding our time, then moved to his table. If we were going to kick off, it was better to be close to a station so we could duck and run. Nothing worse than having the train stop between stations, if that happened the next time the doors opened it would be by the transport police.

Dave sat next to me, and Jason blocked Joe in on the other side.

It was my idea to put a lit cigarette up his nose. Not to burn him, I put it in filter end first. I thought that it would make him snap out of it, but it just hung there. Smoke gently rising before his face like a veil.

Jason rifled through Joe's coat pockets and found an iPod.

Still no reaction.

Jason put it on.

I drank my beer, waiting for a reaction.

That went down slowly. I even opened the next. That was when Joe snapped out of his trance.

If before, no one was home, it was as though a host of people had returned, and turned all the lights on at once. Even the drugs and beer coursing around my system couldn't mask the sickness that rose in my stomach. I knew he was bad news. We'd gone kicking over rocks looking for grass snakes and found a cobra.

Smooth as can be, he coughed softly, took the cigarette out of his nose and then the fucker dropped it in my beer.

Jason's meaty hand clamped over his, smashing it down to the table, and I shouted something along the lines of, what the fuck are you doing. In fact, that's exactly what I shouted. Didn't matter that we'd invaded his space, that I'd stuck a lit fag up his nose.

That's when his watch clattered across the surface top and stopped in front of me.

The gold reflected the light from the window, dancing across my eyes. I saw familiar landmarks of Leeds station reflected in the glass, as the second hand smoothly continued to glide around uninterrupted.

He looked down and twitched. I registered this, snatched it from the table, wondering how I'd managed to beat him.

Only now do I realise that he wanted me to do that.

I took it.

"You don't want that watch," he said.

"Oh, but I do," I said. "It looks expensive."

He didn't say anything to that. The corner of his mouth turned up. Not a smirk, but not a smile either.

"Don't say I didn't warn you." He was so calm. Even though Jason had pinned his hand to the table. It must have been uncomfortable, but he didn't show it.

I know now that it wasn't a threat. It was an offer. It was advice.

The banter flew back and forth for the thirty odd seconds that the train took to finish pulling into the station. I managed to stand in the aisle just as a load of suits were walking past, slipping among them, using them as a barrier. Jason released Joe's arm, and followed. I glanced back and saw Joe take his bag down from the overhead rack, staring at me through the crowd. I made my way off the train.

The suits dispersed as soon as they hit the platform, dragging their Samsonite cases behind.

At this point, I thought that Joe was a bit of a loser, so far we'd only had a bit of verbal from him, and we'd abused him pretty bad. Jason was bopping along to whatever crap was on the iPod. It all changed when he stepped off the train. He'd been noise so far. Insistent, not violent.

The train was at one end of the station, away from the main concourse, out under open air. There was high fence to one side, separating the platform from a twenty-foot drop onto the back streets of Leeds. I should know the name of the building it overlooked - Crown Plaza, or Crown Place. Something. I've been dropped there many a night, stood, bathed in blue neon from the office block, three sheets to the wind, freezing my bollocks off, taking a piss through the fence.

I thought we'd simply walk out of there and that would be the end of it. Not many people start a fight cold. The initial flash point had passed, and Jason seemed subdued by whatever music was currently blasting into his head.

Joe came up behind us, even though he was effectively cornered. He had nowhere to go, unless he wanted to drop onto the track.

I looked at him; one against three.

"Let it lie," I said. Usually this was enough of a warning that anyone with any common sense would walk away. Most of the time they wouldn't even call the cops, just glad that they got out of the situation without a beating.

Belongings can be replaced, faces take longer to heal. Of course, Jason and Dave took him to be someone they could abuse without consequences, especially after what they'd done to his coat.

He didn't seem concerned by the odds, and that should have set alarm bells ringing, but the beer must have dulled my senses.

He didn't seem frightened, anything but.

"Quit following us!" Jason bellowed.

Jason didn't wait for a reply, he took a swing. Usually, that would have been the end of it, Jason's right hook destroys whatever it hits.

Joe blocked it by elbowing him in the bicep, then closed the distance and landed a solid head-butt. My brother toppled, left arm flailing to stop his descent. I heard a crack like a gunshot when he hit the concrete.

Joe bent down and collected his iPod.

"Look, when you're tired of the watch, find me. I'll take it back."

"Fuck you," I said. Frightened at the efficiency in which he'd taken Jason down.

Joe picked up his bag from the platform, and we watched, as he wrote something on a piece of paper. Jason rolled from side to side, trying to clutch his head and arm at the same time.

"Last chance," he said, holding out the note.

"What's that?"

"That's how you can find me."

"What if I don't want to find you?" I replied.

A moment passed. I chewed the inside of my lip, wondering who was going to make the first move. Boxers waiting for the bell to ring.

Joe opened his hands, taking a sideways step. "Have it your way. Whatever happens, never tell him it's after midnight."

"What?"

"You'll find out."

"That's your problem." He shrugged and dropped the note on Jason.

That was the last I saw of him.

I don't know why, but I retrieved the paper.

It was his number and a name, *Joe Mancer.*

What sort of a name was that?

Jason puked at the ticket inspection barrier. His left arm floated below the elbow bending the wrong way when he tried to use it to open the gate. I opened it for him and he sniffed loudly, then said that he was off to A&E.

He jumped the taxi queue.

Dave and me went to Bosco's Emporium.

Forty quid. That was all the tight, cheap bastard gave me.

I tucked ten into my jacket for Jason and gave Dave fifteen. Easy come, easy go. It would get a couple of extra beers.

The watch was now someone else's problem.

"Give us that paper." Dave said.

I passed him the sheet that Joe had written his name on. Dave tore it into strips and wrote, "Joe Mincer - eats cock" with the phone number on each. He laughed. We both found it amusing leaving his details on our travels.

We left them like breadcrumbs wherever we went: outside call boxes, notice boards, and anywhere else we thought some perv might pick one up and give Joe hassle.

At some point during the evening, we ran out money, so Dave went off to lose himself with a different kind of chemical and I was on my own.

I gave Emma, my then girlfriend, a ring; we hooked up half an hour later and headed back to my place. I was very drunk.

Emma clung onto my arm when we arrived back at the

entrance to my building. It took a second or two to focus on the figure that was hunched beneath the bare electric bulb in the atrium. I didn't recognise Bosco at first, his large heavyset frame, grubby clothes that formed a strata rather than regular layers. He stared at me, hooded eyes flaring like nostrils.

He blustered towards me, quicker than I'd given someone of his size credit for. He tore my hand from my pocket and prised my fingers open. "You shit. Don't bring any of this crap to my shop."

I felt sharp edges dig into my palm, and looked down to see the watch.

Was it a dud, fake, or really hot?

"I…" I didn't have any of his money left, even Jason's ten had been spent on chasers. I felt bad, but wasn't sure why. It wasn't as though Bosco had ever been good to me. He'd fleeced me more times than I'd walked away feeling that it had been a fair exchange.

"I'll pay you back," I said, still thinking that I could keep him sweet. I still needed somewhere I could dump stuff.

"You owe me nothing." Bosco stormed off two paces, and then spun on his heel, pointing a stubby finger in my face. "Stay away."

Emma called him a loser. But, with hindsight, I don't know if she was saying that to the right person.

We went straight to my bedroom; I dropped the watch into the top drawer next to my bed while Emma went through her bathroom rituals.

I lay down, listening to the sound of the water running in the sink and passed out.

When I woke, nothing made sense.

Emma was still dressed, boots and all, in bed next to me, squashed against the wall as though I was the local priest. She screamed, "You fucking tell your dad I don't like him watching!"

She pointed to the bedroom door that was wide open. The whole room was shadows, but the dark corridor beyond was just blackness.

I'm sure I closed it before I fell into bed, and she would have come from the en-suite in the adjacent wall.

"What the fuck are you on about, Em? I live alone."

She was crying. "He tried to touch me."

That's the quickest anyone's left my flat. I had to unbolt the door to let her out, and then I spent an uneasy five minutes wandering around my place with a snooker cue expecting the bogeyman to jump me. It was empty, of course.

The day went downhill from there.

I went around to Jason's, to see what time he'd finally got in. My head was sore. I was pissed at Emma, and I needed a distraction. I'd never seen her spooked like that. It couldn't have been paranoia, she rarely touched that stuff nowadays.

Jason wasn't there.

I couldn't find Dave either, which wasn't uncommon. So with nothing to do, I went home to sleep off the hangover from hell.

When I got back to my building, all the residents were outside.

They were watching a stream of creatures leave the building, spiders, flies, moths, creeping and crawling over the threshold. Seeing one or two is normal most days inside the flat, woodlice, spiders, the usual critters. This time it was as though they'd all decided to vacate at once - from the entire building.

I watched for ten minutes.

When I got into my flat. I found that not all the insects had managed to leave. The bedside table was covered in spiders.

They'd not left because they were dead.

I swept the small ones into a bin bag, their legs curled into their bodies so that they looked like raisins. The bigger ones I picked up and dropped out a window. I pulled the bedclothes to make sure that there weren't any in there, itching the whole time.

Before it got dark, I made sure that the flat was absolutely empty. I checked each room, then every lock.

Feeling a little better, with nothing unusual to see. I decided that I'd speak to Emma tomorrow, ask what she thought she saw.

Just before I turned out the light, I happened to glance at the bedside table. There was the watch. I snatched it from the table and dropped it back in the top drawer.

I awoke to pitch-blackness. I couldn't see anything. I mean nothing, not even the outline of the curtains against the streetlights below.

My breath caught in my throat.

It was cold.

I tried to pull the covers up that I'd shrugged off in the night. I pulled on the top of the duvet, but it wouldn't move.

There was weight at the bottom of the bed. I couldn't see, but it was there, in the blackness.

A gruff voice asked, "What time is it?"

I let go, crushing myself back into the corner of the room like Emma had done. Feeling the freezing plaster against my bare back and hearing my own ragged breathing.

I didn't move until light from outside started to poke its way through the window.

On the bedside drawers, the watch was there, facing towards me.

I went looking for Jason. Found him at the hospital. He'd been discharged, his arm now in a cast. He was still there because Dave was up in intensive care. Apparently, the pills that we'd taken the day before had been spiked. He must have had a load more after he left me. His mind was somewhere, free, but his body was stuck on life support.

Feeling sorry for myself, I tried to find Joe's number. I ended up going back through all the places we'd been that night, and even some we didn't. I didn't care about the strange looks I got, asking if anyone had seen a piece of paper with Joe Mincer's number.

I couldn't find any. TransPennine didn't know. No CCTV footage from the station, even the police didn't know where or how I could find him.

That was two weeks ago.

Emma won't have anything to do with me. I saw her once or twice. The first time she saw me she vanished before I could catch up. The second time she pretended she didn't know who I was.

Even Jason doesn't talk to me anymore. He sits at home, watching television. The doctor said that there's a chance his arm won't heal, and if it does, it will never be as strong as it used to be.

Every night the ghost comes. Sometimes quietly, sometimes throwing me across the room. He always asks what the time is. He... he makes me answer, but so far, I've never told him it was later than eleven.

What happens after midnight? I don't want to know. I *so* do not want to find out.

Me, I'm still looking.

If anyone has heard of Joe Mancer, or sees him, tell him I'm sorry. Tell him that I'm looking for him.

Tell him that I have something of his.

Tell him that I have his watch.

SACRIFICE

In five hours, Malcom Burke would be standing in a dark corner of the hospital with the ghost of his daughter in his pocket, waiting to hear whether the surgeon could remove the glass shards from his wife's eyes.

The hours of the afternoon limped along. His continued glances at the clock's hands didn't push them around any quicker and it didn't give him any more ideas on how he might save his dying relationship. Too late each tick taunted, too late; it was making even the good memories feel as though he'd been left holding flowers at his younger self's grave.

His phone vibrated in his pocket. Reluctantly, he took it out. Turning it in his hands, he could see that it was a message from Catherine. The same message she'd been sending every day this month.

How had it come to this?

The resulting sigh blew dust to the furthest corner of his desk.

"I know it's short notice, but you have got to see this. Trust me." Keith's voice drifted over the cubicle wall. Malcom couldn't see who he was talking to. "You'll dig this. I'm so sure - I already bought you both tickets."

Silence. Must be a phone call.

"Not just a medium. The Medium. Jillian Underwood."

The name was familiar, but by obscure infamy rather than by reputation. Malcom's ears pricked.

"Shit."

The phone call was not going well.

"Look man, I'm down eighty on this. Come on." Pause. "I know I should have checked with you first, but I didn't know that it was on. I bought the last tickets at the venue. There won't be another show like it…" Keith's voice took on a pained tone. "Yeah, you're right. I know. I know, but… Okay. Yeah, I guess I could try and sell them." The conversation ended with a defeated 'Bye.'

When Malcom peered over the cubicle, Keith was cradling the phone thoughtfully.

"Hey," Malcom said, an idea already forming. "I just might be able to do you a favour."

He felt buoyed by the tickets. He didn't believe in any of that supernatural hoodoo-voodoo bullshit, but it wasn't about that. It was about finding an angle that was unusual enough so that Catherine wouldn't already have an opinion. He could play up the fact that there would be people there who had also lost someone, people looking for reassurance and comfort. Maybe even other relatives of children affected by the Rose Killer. They were going. Why not? Even if she tore the tickets and threw them at him, at least he'd tried. Last week it would have been money that they couldn't afford, but now it was rapidly losing its value.

After a shaky start trying to convince someone who hadn't left the house in what felt like months, that, not only would they be appearing in public, they had to do so that very evening, Catherine agreed. Understandably, there were a couple of wobbles, a few wardrobe changes, but she trusted him and they made it out of the house.

Despite the air of attending an event, there was always Sarah's shadow that permeated his soul. There was no escaping, but the darkness didn't feel so complete.

Catherine looked amazing, he kept stealing glances at her as he drove into town, not quite believing that the woman next to him wasn't in her uniform grey sweatshirt and jogging bottoms.

At the venue, Malcom's anxiety returned as a young guy scanning tickets, allocating seat numbers walked towards them. With a reader attached to his phone, he scanned their tickets and called out to a colleague behind the counter.

He shrugged as though it was inconveniencing him as much as it was them, "this won't take a minute." But he didn't say what he was checking for.

Malcom lent forward, catching a glimpse of the screen. Keith's booking details popped up. Just text, not images. Why was he feeling guilty? He'd bought the tickets in good faith, was there a no transfer policy?

Then it dawned on him. Information.

"Okay, Mr and Mrs Keith Harrison, sorry to keep you waiting, you're in your allocated seats, row Q, twenty-three and twenty-four."

Once the inspector was out of earshot, Catherine asked, "What was that about?"

If he'd been organising the show, then it made sense to have access to the booking records, perform some social media searches, start to build a picture of the audience. For a two-hour show, all you had to do was research eight people long enough to have a fifteen-minute conversation with each. Everyone not in the know would think it was magic. Or sixty people for two minutes. Hell that would be impressive but for different reasons. Instead Malcom said, "probably for cancellations, moving people closer if they have better seats available."

He wasn't surprised when the next person walking down the line was the star of the show herself. Probably shaking hands and making notes.

Jillian Underwood was an imposing woman, not tall, but confident. Rowdy behaviour calmed in her presence. She was gaunt, with more than a hint of Cruella de Vil, the only thing that ruined the impression was the dark green parker in stark contrast to her ash blond hair. It wouldn't be her coat, most likely borrowed, to add that approachable touch as she mingling with her audience. As if somehow that would disguise her from being recognised as the host once she was on stage.

Listening, she moved up and down the line, shaking hands, striking out with pleasantries and obviously fishing for information. She stopped next to Catherine. Bangles and jewellery chiming in the wind.

The guy who had scanned their ticket joined her. He scanned the ticket once more and then said: "Keith and Emma Harrison."

Jillian shook her head, "They aren't, but it doesn't matter." She reached out and put her hand on Catherine's sleeve. "You need to be close to the stage. Row C, four and five."

"But that's…" her assistant protested.

She only had to glance at him to exert her authority.

"But, they're already in."

"Move them." Jillian hissed.

The house lights dimmed, all but one which intensified on the sharp suited compere.

"Thank you for coming here tonight. My name is Aaron. Before we begin, I would just like to say a couple of words. We are not out to trick you, we're not, what you see tonight is genuine, but like mobile phones, times have changed. In the old days, you would be gathered around a small table, and be listening to someone who was – and I quote 'possessed' - by the spirit of a loved one. Unfortunately, that method was so open to abuse. It's easy to put on a voice and spout nonsense, claiming it to be messages from the other side. Where there's suffering there's money, and where there's money there are fakes.

"While you can't pick up a phone and talk to the dead, we're not that far away."

He let that sink in for a moment. "People change when

they are presented with new information, new evidence. Old beliefs get examined and re-evaluated. In a moment you are going to witness one of the most talented and gifted mediums of our lifetime. For you to make that informed decision, I need to explain what else you are going to see, namely the equipment. It'll help you be able to come to your own conclusion without an outside narrative. You decide where the miracles really come from.

"First we have a light box. Nothing more than that. It has a single light source, like a normal light, but brighter. This is used to create what's known as a volumetric light effect. It's the same thing that happens when light passes through suspended particles. Not unlike a streetlight on a misty evening. Thankfully you won't be asked to move out into the street."

There was a small laugh from the audience.

"What you'll see will be similar to looking at images on a waterfall."

Aaron moved across to the back of the table, where he removed a panel from the side of a metallic box.

"Not many people will know what the inner workings of this equipment should look like, but you can all see there's a bulb and power cables – nothing else, no computer, no receiver, it just spits out concentrated light.

"All of this is behind two large Perspex screens. If anything goes bump, or something breaks, it should all be contained."

Aaron walked to the centre of the stage and gestured to the wings.

"Without much further ado, let me introduce Jillian Underwood!"

She entered to rapturous applause.

She wore an ear piece and microphone. Her voice came from speakers around the room, loud and clear. "Thank you for your warm welcome, thank you Aaron. "Let me get this straight. This is not entertainment. This is not entertaining."

The auditorium fell silent.

"I ask that you respect those around you. Bereavement is not entertainment. If anyone here thinks that it is, leave. If you go now, you will be entitled to claim a full refund."

She waited for a moment. No one moved, other than a few members of the audience who lent forwards enraptured by her spell.

Jillian clasped her hands together. "Thank you. You've decided to stay. Relax, if you can. Open your mind, and most of all don't judge. If you see anything upsetting, turn away. If you hear anything too disturbing, ear protectors can be found under each seat.

The central light dimmed and the glass screens flickered to life. Sounds hissing from the ether through speakers.

There was nothing. Only noise. Then light. Blinking snowflakes of interference. It too faded. Jillian's head rolled forwards and her arms spasmed like the legs of a hanged man.

Slowly, out of the shifting darkness came the distorted image of a child. A girl, long hair falling over her face and although it was just her outline.

"Oh God." Whispered Catherine. It was Sarah.

Malcom's stomach heaved. Their daughter was lost within a frame. Drawn by bright light, detailed enough to see the single chicken pox scar on her forehead. Catherine's nails dug into the palm of his hand.

He looked at his wife, at the tears starting to streak down her face.

This was a snapshot into somewhere else, a world of misery and pain. She was crying, looking over her shoulder. The flash of the whites of her eyes made her look like a trapped animal.

There was someone else as well. Footsteps echoed from the glass although he couldn't see. A door slammed at the back of the theatre and the noise came out of the speakers like a gunshot.

Malcom swallowed, or tried to, his tongue stuck to the rough of his mouth. On stage Sarah started to panic. There was a soft snap followed by a hiss of leather and a low menacing growl. Even before the shadow appeared over their daughter's shoulder, that of a man wrapping a belt around his fist. Catherine was out of her seat, moving swiftly down the aisle. The photograph of her killer that appeared in the papers after his death failed to capture the sheer menace and presence the predator stood behind her radiated.

"Oh fuck." His legs felt like stilts as he tried to follow in his wife's wake. The churn of feet and bags and people made it impossible to catch up.

Jillian shouted a warning.

Catherine had already pushed aside the first safety screen and was reaching out to the glass box for Sarah.

Someone in the audience screamed.

The image of their daughter exploded.

Shrapnel and debris ricocheted from moved barriers, ripping into the audience. Catherine caught the full force of the blast, her face a pin cushion of glass splinters. Malcom was far enough away to get a hand in front of his face, his palm peppered with fine needles. A fragment, two feet long, impaled the man to his left and it was his flailing arm that caught Malcom across the side of his head, knocking him to the floor.

The world shifted. In the end there was darkness.

Under the red emergency lights, the floor glistened like frost covered fields. It was chaos, people cried, screamed, and called to one another. On the floor, the glass reflected what little light there was. For a second he thought that he could see shapes moving upon the shattered surfaces.

Pushing himself up with an elbow, using the padding of his jacket as protection, he managed to get to his knees. By his left, before his shadow fell across a shard. He saw Sarah staring up, hands pressed against the miniature window, banging to be let out.

Malcom put it into his pocket, then fought to get to Catherine.

He'd cradled her hand in the crook of his wrists all the way to the hospital, deaf to the siren's wailing and the motion of the ambulance. A nurse had prised him away, then removed the splinters in his own hands, eventually leading him to a waiting area where the injured congregated. Wherever he looked, it was bloodied suits and shredded evening wear.

It was there that Aaron found him.

"You were with that woman who ran into the glass?" Aaron said. It wasn't accusatory, but still it caused a few heads to turn. Aaron motioned to him, "Come with me."

Malcom followed.

The two men walked deeper into the hospital, until the only people they passed in corridors were staff.

At last he stopped at a door and stepped inside.

Jillian waited, perched on the end of the bed. Her arm was in a sling and her dress was decorated with black blooms of dried blood.

"Mr...?" She stumbled for a name.

"Malcom."

"Yes, yes. How is Catherine?"

"She's in surgery, I don't know. Look can you help us?"

"That depends, it's obvious that the girl is your child. Do you know who the man was behind her?"

"That was the Rose Killer. Kendrick Murphy. He took her away from us, and twelve others."

Jillian shook her head.

Malcom felt his stomach being sucked down into his shoes.

"I'm sorry." Jillian said. "I had no idea that she was still in danger. I wouldn't have continued if I had known."

"There's also this." Malcom said, and he removed the

glass from his pocket.

"Oh my!" Jillian exclaimed.

"May I?" Aaron gently took the piece and held it up to the light.

Sarah patiently looked down upon them.

"Can you help me save my daughter?"

"No. I can't."

"What do you mean you can't? Isn't there anything you can do?"

"I am sorry, Malcom. I can't."

"You can't just leave her like this! You did this to her!"

"No Malcom. Your wife did this. She…"

"Was only trying to get her to safety. Isn't there anything, anyone?" Malcom pleaded.

Aaron shook his head. "Jillian can only communicate with the dead, she can't do anything more than that."

"I'm begging you! Please!"

"There is… there is one." Jillian had already taken out her mobile and was dialling a number.

When it started to ring, she held it across to Malcom.

"When Joe answers, tell him who you are." Jillian shrugged, "He won't talk to me."

"Who is he?"

"He's my son."

There was a sharp click, a hiss of static and then "Hello?" Malcom didn't know what history they had, even whether he trusted her, but what choice did he have?

"Hello Joe, my name is Malcom Burke, I'm here with Jillian." He tried to moisten his lips, but couldn't, instead the water he tried to summon poured from his eyes. A grown man crying into a phone. The piece of glass vibrated in his pocket as Sarah moved.

Again, there was a pause, then "Malcom, where are you?"

Mercifully, Aaron took the phone from him. "We're at the Imperial Hospital. We're in ward seven. Room three-oh-five... Where are you?"

Static. A voice cutting out, fading from far away.

"He's gone."

Malcom stared at the phone.

The door burst inwards.

"Here." In the harsh lights of the hospital room, Joe looked like a shadow that had pulled itself from the darkness and defied the light to stand wherever he pleased. His outline was indistinct. Looking closer Malcom saw droplets of water fall to the floor, as ice crystals that clung to Joe's coat melted. Joe was dropping something into his pocket, his phone.

The newcomer glanced at Jillian but addressed Aaron. "Is she okay?"

Aaron nodded.

"What happened?"

After they told him everything. Malcom showed him his daughter.

"This is the safest place for her right now. As long as she is in there, she's not in any immediate danger."

"Can you help?" Malcom asked.

"Maybe. How far are you willing to go?"

Malcom looked into the eyes of his dear daughter, seeing her face brighten in response. "Whatever needs to be done. No matter the cost. Anything."

Joe nodded. "Okay. I'll need to do a few things first. You make sure that your wife's okay. Give me your number. It'll take a couple of days. You need to be ready to do what I say."

A few days later Joe called, asking for five thousand pounds to be transferred to his account. He didn't say why.

What could he do? If felt like a set-up. Some fiction manufactured to inflict the most pain from the suffering. The piece of glass with his daughter, moving around inside, seemingly alive. Could he risk not taking the chance?

"How long will it be?" Malcom asked.

"A few more days. I promise." Joe said.

Only it wasn't.

Two months later.

Two months with living with the image of your daughter trapped within a macabre ornament. Knowing that you've been scammed. Two months where no one returned his calls, and with letters from the bank questioning why there wasn't enough funds to cover day-to-day payments. Two months for the hate to build and then subside.

Catherine was home, sitting in the living room listening to the television. Her eyes had been saved, but they wouldn't know how badly her vision had been affected until next month when the bandages were removed.

The phone rang.

Malcom glanced at it. Not equipped for any more demands.

"Are you going to get that?" Catherine asked.

Reluctantly he did.

Malcom recognised the voice on the other end of the line.

"Malcom? Sorry it's been so long; I've been... busy. Can't talk. Do you still have Sarah?"

"Joe! Yes. Yes. We do."

"A lot has happened, and I understand you may feel some resentment toward me. I apologise, but it was unavoidable. I am, I'm sorry about that. If there had been a way to get a message to you, I would have done so. Anyway, I need you to take the fragment and smash it. Wrap it into a pillowcase, or towel. Something to keep it all together and then break it as small as possible. Grind it to dust if you can."

"But…"

"She'll be fine. Trust me. It will release her."
"What about the other?"
"… I've taken care of him."
"What happens now?"
"You know you said that you'd do anything for her?"
"Yes."
"Do you still feel the same way? Would you change anything?"
"No."
"After you break the glass, I'll collect you. We're not done yet. What happens next is on your shoulders."
"Okay."
"Oh, and I'm ashamed to have to ask this, but I need another thousand."

Malcom went out behind the garage with a sack and a hammer.

He was shaking with anger so much that it took him four attempts hit the glass.

He had a dream that night. A crazy dream where it all made sense at the time. Joe was there. Bank notes floated out of his pockets vanishing into the sky like smoke.

They were looking for Sarah, walking out of town through waste ground. It was dark, and the grass was so cold against his feet that the blades burned.

"What are we doing?" he asked.

"Bringing Sarah home."

They walked beneath a faded moon, against trees that scratched at the sky and howled at their passing.

Finally, Joe bent down, "Come closer. This is where Sarah is."

Malcom looked at the ground, there was nothing there, just dirt and stones and leaves. He placed his hands on the ground, feeling the loamy soil beneath his fingers.

"There's no guarantee, only risk. And hope." Joe smiled.

All doubt left Malcom, questions about the money,

what he'd done with it. At that point in time he felt sure that it was the right thing to do.

"It's not like pouring life out from one container to another – it doesn't work like that. It might kill you, it might not. One thing for sure, it's going to change you forever. Last chance to back down. You sure you still want to do this?"

"Yes! More than anything."

"You sure?"

Malcom felt a hand on his shoulder. Then so much pain he thought that he was dying.

Catherine's vision never fully recovered, she was partially sighted in her right eye and colour blind and short sighted in her left.

Malcom simply sat on the settee, looked out of the window, and waited. The day transitioned from stage to stage like the phase of the moon, all the while he listened to the stillness of the house. Catherine did the same. Her breathing giving her away, occasionally her hand would find his, and they would lock fingers, clenched together in joint prayer. Hours would pass, their house an oasis of silence in the sea of everyday normality.

Finally, he would let go of Catherine, easing his fingers from her grip. She resented him breaking the illusion, turning away. It was obvious that they were alone and that the world was moving on without them.

Through the window, he saw Joe appear by the front gate, watched him stumble with something he was carrying.

Not something - someone.

Joe's movement was slow, arduous.

Malcom stood, surprised at the effort needed. His limbs limp by his side unresponsive.

Joe wavered.

Malcom peered out of the living room window,

noticing that Joe had changed. Diminished.

There was a girl in his arms. Malcom could see her hair, golden in the sunlight, caught in a breeze.

Joe put her down then lent against the post for support.

Malcom coughed and pain exploded in his chest. Sharp, like he'd eaten a handful of fish hooks and each one had snagged on the inside of his ribs. When he looked again, Joe had gone.

He wiped the back of his hand across his lips, tasting copper. His hand came away red, wet.

There were little footsteps that pattered along the pavement towards the door. An envelope dropped through, splitting as it hit the mat. A slew of twenty pound notes spilled across the welcome mat. It wasn't the banknotes that drew his attention the most, it was the tiny fingers that had waved through the flap.

His view was blocked by Catherine as she moved through from the kitchen. She glided down the hallway, her fingers brushed along the walls for guidance. When she opened the door, it took a second to realise that her scream was one of joy.

He cried.

He couldn't help it. His vision clouded and dizziness washed over him in waves. After a moment the sensation passed.

Malcom wiped his eyes, feeling as though he had stepped out from under a cloud.

Then he went outside to join his wife and daughter.

LUCIFER'S REDEMPTION

What can happen in an instant?
A heartbeat.
A blink.
A quickening of the pulse.
An inhalation expanding your lungs, ready to carry a scream past your lips as darkness fills your vision.

Lives can change in an instant. A car mounting the pavement can tear a hole in the universe. A tragedy that adds an unexpected full stop at the end of a family's existence. This had happened to me. Left me crippled, derailed and full of hate.

I hated myself: for surviving, for what I had become and for who I was before. How shallow and insignificant my thoughts and emotions were. That the worst injustices I had to suffer were early bedtimes and being told to tidy up the toys that I'd strewn across the floor before getting more out of the box. How I despised my father's hand on my shoulder, guiding me up the stairs to bed, and now how I would have almost done anything to feel his touch again.

The caretaker had positioned my wheelchair beneath the attic hatch. He couldn't think of an easy way to get me up into the overhead crawlspace so he gently shut me in a case and carried me up as though I was another piece of baggage. We all were. Complicated lives with pasts that couldn't be rewritten.

I listened to the soft zip as the case was opened and found myself in the attic.

As I was lifted out, I nodded my gratitude.

The caretaker smiled. "Don't worry too much about making a mess, just keep the noise down. Ring the bell when you've finished, if I don't hear anything I'll be back in an hour." He removed the kitchen bell from his overalls and placed it within reach near the hatch, then vanished.

The rest of the boarded space had been taken up with shallow piles of bags and boxes. Some had already been moved from their original positions so that I could crawl my way around and look in without too much assistance. This was far more than I'd expected.

Histories lay scattered around the dusty eaves. Each suitcase, holdall, or box contained fragments of previous lives. Mine was here too, buried amongst past, forgotten things. We weren't allowed to keep them with us. Not one single memento. Everything was taken from us, pared down and stored. When I first came here, I went through the remnants of my previous life with a stranger who held up my photos like flash cards.

I was made to decide what to discard.

Then once I'd had my heart wrenched, and I thought that I'd finished, they made me go through the entire process again.

And then again, a month later.

They wanted me to forget.

Only I didn't want to.

A small case had been put up in the attic when I first arrived. I was sure that there would be a few loose photos in there.

Maybe one of us together.

I glanced at the hatch, hearing the world below filter through.

It took time, moving around the boarded roof space. I had to use my good arm to drag myself from place to place leaving trails in the dust, but the boxes were of a level that once I'd worked my way over to them I could go through their contents without too much difficulty.

I started looking. Time ticked away.

The faded blue case - it wasn't here.

My heart sank.

The glimmer of who I once was had been extinguished. Leaving a phantom, standing in blackness, stretching to infinity. There was nothing to hold me to the past the image that I had of them in my head was already becoming blurred at the edges.

I was like most children, too caught up wanting the next distraction, rather than taking the time to appreciate who looked after me. Thrilled for the experiences they provided, but when had I ever been grateful?

I'd almost given up hope. Every muscle ached even the missing ones. My nose and throat clogged with dust.

Then I saw it. I'd been here long enough that the light falling through the skylight had shifted along the boards and now fell on a pile that I'd discarded earlier having not recognising any of the bags there. I saw my case through a hole in another.

Fatigue gave way to hope and I rolled to the stack. I reached through the small hole to touch the handle within.

A tingle ran the length of my good arm, across my frail chest and into my withered left. The sensation was invasive, foreign to that limb, triggered by touching the bag. It didn't feel good. My chest tightened, and I felt my entire body thump with each heartbeat. I wondered what had been hidden from me since I'd arrived at the orphanage.

I pushed the items stacked on top and they slid away.

The outer case was battered brown leather, fastened by

large buckles that fought with my fingers as I undid them.

Opening my case was easy. The zip flew around the outside of the blue checked material as though it was opening itself dragging my hand around with it.

Inside was a single ornate box. The surface of the dark wood was covered with markings not unlike tattoos.

This was mine. More important to me than mere possessions, but I couldn't remember why.

There was a sound. Indistinct. Like the chatter of voices, or teeth. I took it to be noises from the outside playground, carried to the eaves and conducted through the vents.

The box shivered as I held it, my hand feeling the shifting weight from one side of the box to the other.

Rats, maybe? Mice?

But the case was sealed, whatever was in there had to have been there all along.

Still, using the tips of my fingers, I carefully opened it. The case awned like a mouth, ready to snap shut.

Light cascaded from the opening, touching me with its harsh caress.

Projected within the light were figures of familiar ghosts, acting out scenes that played on the sloped attic walls.

My shock and amazement was short lived. But, pain followed. The harsh anguish of realisation. A brightness like quicksilver ran over my hand, burning its way to my soul.

I was wrong.

This was the very thing that I'd been trying to escape: the essence of my thoughts and memories distilled.

I had been yearning to remember a past. To retain who I was.

So I'd found my past. Not the immediate past, but all the pasts that I'd ever lived.

This was a revelation. It was like asking for a glass of water only to be dropped into the ocean.

I didn't want this. The spectrum of my perception went supernova.

God exists.

Tears streamed down my face. Not from joy or spiritual awakening - but shame.

There is a God all right, and he hates me.

My memories fused, streaming into my mind, each emotion as fresh and clear as the moment they were etched there the first time.

An explosion ripped through my senses and I was shredded by the debris. My past lives fused with me, and I relived them all.

I was falling.

Falling faster than a meteor.

The ground was coming up to greet me, rotating around me as though it was a giant fly circling my head; until it started to fill my vision.

My bones would be broken and limbs pulped; my innards scoured across the landscape in one long bloody streak.

Landmarks became distinct, mountains, lakes, fields. Then the colours broke apart into more definition, rock faces, forests, eventually trees. I became frightened – how could I survive?

I gritted my teeth and closed my eyes. As much protection as screaming my sanity away.

The impact was worse than I'd imagined.

It took a while for the boiling thoughts to return to their rightful places.

They simmered, but eventually the bubbling settled down to a semblance of calmness. The rawness was as fresh as my tears.

I sniffed loudly. Relieved that it was only a memory, but also upset that I was back where I started. The echoes of the false life fell, the new point of view overriding the old.

I had done this to myself.

My name is Lucifer. I am the devil.

Swirling motes danced through the evening sunlight, spilling impassively beneath the supporting beams. Beautiful, and yet sinister; He had a hand in this. He was probably watching now, laughing as I suffered.

There was no point maintaining the disguise, the assumed identity shed easily like tipping a hat. The body felt fragile; it was. I had been trapped within the skeletal prison of a cripple, but even then I managed to be reunited with my memories. Or rather they had sought me out, conveniently presenting themselves in a box, stowed alongside the remnants of the other children's previous lives and keepsakes.

There was nothing else for it, but to admit defeat and go home.

I didn't fall, I was thrown.
A child dashed against a round wall.

It was that moment that I've been trying to forget.
Forget who I was, what I'd done.
But in the end, it wasn't possible.
My own black thoughts took me back to Hell, where I became lost once more.

For a long time I wandered through the landscapes of my domain, my inner voice eloquent with self-loathing and despair.

My fortified manor house in Limbo stood alone and forlorn. I journeyed there, rested against the wrought iron fence that surrounded the land, but went no further. By the front gates were lines of tortured spirits, those seeking to petition their ruler for a decree. They gathered seeking penance. In the past I'd metered out decisions, supposedly weighing suffering against sin and directing the ghosts to their next destination, but it was all the same. They were like me, trying to escape the burden of their wrongdoing, but nothing changed.

Hell could rule itself.

It had until now, and would endure still.

I walked to get away from myself, lost in recollections of my failings. One memory linking to several more and so on until a network of guilt consumed my mind.

I fled and became just another old tortured soul.

There was no night, no day. Not that it mattered. The environment around me didn't change who I was. Like the transient footprints I left behind, soon to be filled with dust. Beyond the immediate, it was as though I'd never existed here.

Columns of black smoke rose from burning rents, streaming into a sky the colour of an old bruise.

I walked through the ash covered landscape, forever.

… But that was not to be my fate.

"Lucifer?" The voice was a whisper, barely audible above my laboured breathing. My thoughts stuttered. Had it been a memory? A phantom of my past.

There was nothing here. My surroundings shifting dunes, punctured by sporadic rock formations.

"Lucifer…"

There it was again.

I stopped.

I could feel the fine powder shift beneath my feet, so that I sank to the rock beneath.

"Who is it?" I asked. The last word caught in my throat, tripping from cracking lips.

"Lucifer. Is… is that you?" I recognised that voice, one that haunted me in my darkest dreams.

"Yes." I replied, looking around. A memory stirred like gentle ripples across the surface of a lake.

I'm not sure how long I'd been walking. Years? Decades maybe? Trapped within my own past, but now this voice had jolted me back to the present. A chance to be in the moment.

In the shallow of a dune, a hole had been cut into a rock, making a small cave.

Only, it wasn't a cave, it was a cell.

The shape of a hand rose from between two stone columns and collapsed, billowing dust into the air.

I was acutely aware of where I was. How the oppressive colour of the sky leeched optimism, and how my feet chaffed against the inside of my shoes. While the abrasive wind scraped my exposed flesh, guilt and shame seeped into my blood, sweeping quickly around my limbs like poison, robbing me of my strength.

"You came back." The weakness in the voice couldn't disguise his relief.

I had, but not intentionally.

I was also two thousand years too late.

A sigh left my chest, taking with it all the trivial, pretty transgressions that I'd ever committed. Even the most heinous despicable act I'd ever committed was but a candle compared to this inferno.

I deserved the hatred, every bit of it.

And more. I fell to my knees, scrabbling to the bars.

It was Jesus Christ.

Half his beard burnt away, face as weathered as the rocks that imprisoned him. There was only enough room for him to lie in his cell. His face barely above the creeping greyness that threatened to consume him.

He blinked. His perfect blue eyes made all the more striking against the desiccated husk of his face.

As his head lolled forward, one hand opened, his fingers trembled and I realised that he was trying to touch me.

He was here because I had put him here.

Left, like a broken toy soldier at the bottom of a child's toy box.

The sky around me felt heavier, as though it could crush me with the force of a singularity. That or holy fire.

I reached to clasp his hands.

I thought I was all out of tears, but I was wrong.

I didn't apologise, though it was there in my heart. I'd assumed that, being who he was, he'd got out. There had been rumours to that effect. I had no reason to come back. It wasn't my fault.

Then I remembered, I'd started the rumours.

"I'll get you out of here." I said.

The stone bars crumbled beneath my fists.

I'd not found his other hand, so instead grabbed him by the scruff of the neck. It took hardly any effort to pull him out. That's when I realised why I couldn't find his other hand, there wasn't one to find.

It and his legs had burned away.

Desensitised as I was, I felt sick.

A crack of thunder pealed in the distance.

Another memory evoked - this one to do with the mechanics of Hell. It wasn't thunder, but the sound of the Horde being unleashed. These demons were set free when wards were broken, like breaking a seal or cracking a rune. Hell had a way of keeping it's prisoners. Escape was impossible. Despair can always be made the more bitter once it had been tainted by dollop of hope. The denizens would flood over the plains devouring anything in their path.

For the first time I felt a shiver of apprehension. I'd seen the foul creatures at work before, but never anticipated that I'd be the one trying to outrun them.

I wrapped Jesus in my cloak, and cradled him in my arms. Our faces were so close that I could feel the shallow breath on my cheek. What remained of his body made him lighter than an infant.

"I forgive you," he said.
Bastard.

I ran and the Hordes of Hell followed.

There was no one else to blame.

I could feel the sharp stones biting into the soles of my shoes, each time my feet sank beneath the powdery surface. A wake of dust lifted in my trail, drifting upwards marking the sky with our passage.

Jesus slept. Mumbling and pleading when in his sleep with each jolt. He flinched, whimpered and sometimes cried. Silent tears leaked from his eyes. At other times his breathing so quiet that I thought that he'd died and I was carrying his corpse.

By the waters of the Styx, I lay him down and tried to wash away the foulness that caked his body. It also gave me a chance to think what to do next.

The brackish water was alive, no sooner had I cupped my submerged hands I could feel the parasitic worms bumping against my skin trying to find entrance.

Drinking the water would steal memories. Again another fragment of my past returned. This was how I'd tried to forget. I could remember the gritty taste of the liquid as I swallowed. For anyone else it would have been permanent.

I could do that again, maybe if we both drank, the demons that followed wouldn't know who we were. Or I could leave him here.

Any other time, I would have. The easiest action to lie him in the water, let him sink beneath, then drink my fill.

But, this was now.

Hell's an unconventional place, but there are a couple of stationary exits that I know of, gates through to the paradise ruined by mankind. One lay ahead in the City of Dis. Not far from here. So that's where I headed.

Behind a few lost souls wandered the bank, keeping

their distance.

Placing a hand against the stones on the shore. I closed my eyes, reaching through the cold surface to sense what lay around us.

I could hear thoughts, effervescent on the wind. Full of ravenous hate.

Legion.

I couldn't see any of the demons chasing us, but I could hear, and that meant that they wouldn't be far away. Gibbering wails and howls called out from the shadows. They were herding us along a certain direction.

While I could continue indefinitely, this pace was likely to kill Jesus. I tried to carry his as gently as I could, but it was either carry him loosely so that each stride didn't shake his wounds open, or hold him tightly and hope not to crush the life from him.

I had to take it slower, and that gave those creatures following chance to catch up.

Before I could start, a lesser demon, a man shaped like a wolf stepped onto the path in front of us. His thoughts betrayed him, bold, but unsure why he should be frightened of me.

I pinched the life out of the creature with my mind. The body collapsed joint by joint and lay still.

A cry went up in the darkness.

They knew that I was back. By the end of the hunt, one way or another Hell would have a new ruler.

The darkness erupted with movement. Closing in.

I ran.

"They won't let us go," Jesus whispered.

I followed the outline of the river. The surface of the water writhing with silvered forms breaking the surface. Tentacles rolling against each other. There was a Leviathan in there. If Jesus saw it, he didn't say.

Two more wolf-men peeled away from the pack trying

to cut us off.

Again they dropped before they could get within fifty feet. Last spasms escaping their limbs as I stepped over them.

Four more. Same again.

Six. This time, when I stepped over the last it wasn't yet dead. Sharp claws dug into my calf, tearing easily through cloth, skin, and muscle.

I stumbled, leaving it's bleeding corpse, the pain great, but my determination greater.

It wasn't until my leg refused to move at all that I realised it was more serious than I'd thought.

Willpower is all well and good, but there has to be a vessel able to withstand the punishment in order to reach the finish line. I'd not even got close to the outer walls of Dis.

Snarling creatures started to form a circle. Wary since they knew who I was and what I could do, but not intimidated enough to back down.

A coldness seeped into my leg through the wounds frothing lips; it had little blood left to vomit and simply dribbled. I snarled. The ruler of Hell reduced to that of a dog baring its teeth.

"What are they waiting for?" Jesus rasped.

The water parted. From the depths of the Styx a gigantic tentacle emerged. The pointed tip the size of a small mountain, covered with venomous barbs.

"A Leviathan." I said.

As foretold, the end of time would result in Satan's death.

The huge arm seemed ponderous, rising up, up into the sky, blotting out the black smoking columns until the tip reached through the clouds.

A shock ran through me. I knew what crushed bones felt like.

I gritted my teeth. No need to tell Jesus that he was about to be a swatted fly. This was going to hurt. A lot.

The air above my head started to vibrate.

I jumped at the explosion, there was no better word to describe it. The sound of a giant hand slapping a mountain. Chunks of black flesh rained down from the sky and I knew what had happened.

I'd created my own ghost and a figment of Jesus, and sent them to their doom. I also added a reciprocal glamour that turned any aggression back against the attacker. If the attacker had impaled me with a sword - the sword blade would have entered my chest to emerge out of his. Anything more than that, well. Let's say that the Leviathan would at least be one arm down until it grew another.

The deception has served its purpose, hopefully it was enough.

Somewhere in the darkness what remained of my broken ghost, would be shifting from rock to rock to make its way back to me.

There are multiple portals in this realm. The one in Dis is common knowledge, a glittering arch surrounded by guardians. Then, there's another back in my manor. It was there that we returned.

I lost another shadow along the way, I set it across the Infinite Plain, leading a pack of wolf-men. If it remained ahead of the pack, it would run forever.

Finally, I burst through my manor's doors. Moving swiftly through the grand rooms.

Down the hallway, past the set of alcoves, left through a dining room, around the back to a servant's corridor, downstairs…

Into the portal's chamber.

The portal was disguised as painting of rolling hillsides, a simple trick distorted perspective to make it look abstract.

I gently put Jesus down. He coughed softly.

Removing the frame, I didn't hear the visitor step out of the alcove, until the sound of slow clapping reached my ears.

A slow quarter turn and I saw the archangel Michael: His celestial being so bright that it flooded the chamber with brilliant light.

"Well done. I'm impressed. How much of yourself did you sacrifice to get him here?"

I said nothing.

"You think it's slight, three, or four what do you call them, fragments?"

I nodded.

"How many the time before that? And the time before that? And what about all the times that you didn't make it here? How much of yourself have you sacrificed Lucifer?"

"What are you talking about?"

"You'll figure it out soon enough."

"What are you here for Michael?"

"I'm here for his sake. You can't take him through." A ray of light illuminated the portal's frame.

"Are you going to stop me?"

"No."

"Are you going to help me?" I asked.

"No."

"Okay, so what the fuck are you here for?"

"A warning."

I moved closer to the prone form of Jesus, but Michael stepped in the way. We were equal height. We'd fought before. Last time there wasn't much between us, but what had he said about me losing part of myself? What if he was right, what if all the attempts to forget who I was had left part of me behind, that I wasn't strong enough to defeat him. I didn't have time for any of this.

"What is it?" I snapped.

"Why do you think that no one has come for him before now?"

I didn't know. It didn't make sense. I'd not thought

about that. Or maybe I had and forgotten.

Michael continued, "Why leave your only son trapped in Hell? If it had been me, I would have done anything in my power to get him back. I mean two thousand years is a long time."

"Yes, but…"

"Have you asked yourself, why hasn't he been missed?"

"No. But…"

What was Michael saying? Sure he was missed, but they couldn't get to Hell, could they? Michael blew that argument. He was here. What if no one came looking for him because they didn't realise he hadn't returned in the first place?"

Jesus Harrowed Hell prior to his resurrection. But if he didn't return, then had another spirit returned in his place? Dismas, the criminal who had been crucified alongside could have done that. Quite a promotion.

"You've not said anything, other than ask questions, what sort of a warning is it?" I said.

"It's one that you already know." Michael replied. "I am here but to repeat myself for eternity. There is nothing but misery and pain for you. Do not cross the portal." With that the angel vanished.

Would I have done it any other way?

Once more I picked up the ruined body of Jesus and ran toward the portal.

Above, I could hear the demons break down the doors. The shattering glass of windows and their claws strike marbled floors.

The temperature changed as I entered the dimensional door, the grass stretched out to be at the end of a tunnel. Jesus cried out.

My feet carried me faster and faster.

The body in my arms was getting lighter, thinner so that it felt I was carrying air.

"Stop! Stop!" Jesus wept.

He was bleeding again.

I dropped down, trying to staunch the gushing injuries, but I didn't have enough hands. With my bloody fingers, I tried to hold his veins together, keep them from rupturing, but his flesh kept disintegrated beneath my grasp. All his wounds open, the blood loss catastrophic.

I'd emerged onto a sun drenched hillside with a half mangled corpse. There was nothing that I could do to stop it falling apart, staining the grass red.

My howl of raw emotion shattered my ears. The vegetation around me blackened and died. The sound of moving traffic in the distance stuttered with metallic shrieks and squeals of tyres. Birds dropped dead in flight, raining around me.

This was the end of everything.

Of all the eventualities, I wasn't prepared for this. I could have handled a war against heaven's impostor. I could have gone on hunted by both angels and demons. I didn't care what happened to me, I just wanted to put this one thing right. Not for me but for all Jesus had suffered.

This would be a life without end. I am Hell and Hell is me.

Falling to the floor, I screamed.

Cursing myself and damning everyone and everything.

I wept for a very long time.

Whoever said that crying is good for the soul has never lost theirs.

I'd just killed the son of God.

I remained next to the blood soaked ruin, not recognisable as anything that had been living.

I tore at my wrists with my teeth, biting deep to the bone, but even before I could spit out the skin and muscle, my forearms knitted themselves back together. I couldn't die!

How could I go on? Can't forget, can't escape - in mind

or in death? What option was left for me?

I stood, a bloody phantom of defeat, dripping with Christ's blood.

A light pierced the sky, enveloping me.

I couldn't see. Blinded. If I squinted I could make out figures, lots of them. The closest had a sword, or weapon in his hands - a staff?

I tried to shield my eyes, but no matter how I turned, the light was always there.

"Stop." It was his voice.

"Is... is that you? I can't see you." I said.

"Do you need to see me to believe it's me?"

"No, but where are you?"

It was Jesus. Whole and complete. How was this even possible?

"I was never there."

"What?"

"I was never in Hell. Just as you never left. This is your Hell. All of this creation is for you."

"What!?"

"There are only so many times you can walk in a circle before you realise that it is a spiral. This torture has to end. It can go on no longer." Jesus said.

I was overcome with emotion once more. Relief, disbelief, all of it washed down my face.

"Take my hand," He said.

Strong fingers entwined mine.

"What do I do now?"

"Will you follow me?" He asked.

"I will." I said.

"Anywhere?"

"Yes," I replied. "but where are we going?"

"Brother," he said, "I'm here to take you home."

SOUTH COVE

The whole atmosphere was that of a festival, encouraged by the clever arrangement of brightly coloured shop awnings and the jumble of parasols and deckchairs that decorated the streets towards the waterfront. The ambient clutter gave the impression of a parade about to happen.

Eddy slowed long enough to munch through three donuts, then proceeded to pull David in a zigzag from one shop window to another, marking the toys that caught his attention with greasy hand prints on the glass. David happily went with the flow, feeling the hot gritty grasp from his son's hand.

The buildings petered out the further down the sloped road they went, until there was only a hut with stacked windbreaks and plastic chairs where the tarmac frayed into the sand. The imposing cliff face backed the shops, and arced across the land like a giant bite taken from the coast. At the base of the rocks, there was enough room for a single width road that allowed access to the central peninsula, a concrete splinter that stretched out a quarter of a mile into the sea, where it widened to a plateau.

David was a little disappointed that the old lighthouse, still prominent on postcards, was no longer there – though some enterprising ice cream seller had managed to get his van all the way to the very end.

The bucket they brought with them had plenty of uses

that morning. Making castles and towers; using the round bottom to imprint the outline of smiley faces, and eventually for storing small fish, shrimps and crabs that were left stranded in rock pools. Eddy's enthusiasm waned when a baby crab nipped his palm, and every find after that he'd simply clench his hand, shriek and point, wanting David to tease them into captivity. David continued for half an hour, until he was sure that the bucket contained as close to one of everything that could possibly be trapped in a shallow pool, and then found a good excuse to empty the hapless creatures back into the shallows. Eddy stood at the divide where the sand was damp, but not wet, while David washed the bucket out. That was good, David thought, his son knew not to paddle without holding his hand.

One eye on his son, the other on the partly submerged bucket, he smiled. Sunlight prickled his back through his cotton shirt, and ice cold water lapped at his feet. David looked out to sea; blue above and blue below. There was something about the vastness, just being able to see the curvature of the earth out of the corner of his eyes, mind mentally completing the circle and beginning to comprehend the dimensions. First two, then three, then David's eyes were drawn upwards. After being faced with comparisons of such a grand scale and the emptiness of the universe, it followed that his mind turned to something that he could affect. His stomach hadn't started to growl yet, but pre-empting the inevitable would be a good thing. After a couple of hours in the sun it was time to top up their UV protection and rehydrate. The ice cream van on the peninsula would be their next stop.

At regular intervals along the narrow walkway, signs declared 'deep water' with a picture of a sheer drop. Exposed as they were, they had been reinforced against wind and wave by heavy bases, either sandbagged or inserted into large steel discs. David pointed the warning out to Eddy, putting his arm around his shoulder as they peered over the side. Eddy lent back against his father, not wanting to get too close.

"No," Eddy said. "I can see from here."

After a short wait, the queue being processed with ruthless efficiency, they were served.

With melting lolly and ice cream, David and Eddy started the slow shuffle back to the soft sand, dancing from foot to foot to avoid dripping cream or juice on their feet.

"Look, a shark!" Eddy called. "I'll get it, Daddy."

There wouldn't be a shark, not a real one anyway, and if there was, David was sure that the shark would be a plastic toy, left discarded in the sand by another child.

At first David thought that Eddy might have been talking while eating, the words had the same muffled quality. Eddy had been walking alongside him, and it was a shock to realise that he wasn't still in step.

Eddy wasn't pointing to the sand, a small toy, or even out to sea, he was stood arm, at two o'clock to the horizon.

Everything slowed.

Eddy's intense eyes beneath furrowed brows, the pitch of his voice deepened two octaves as he asked "See?" The corner of his son's mouth twitched, but whatever words wanting to be formed weren't externalised. Instead, head tilted back, Eddy stepped forwards, over the low wall towards the edge of the walkway. David's jaw became slack, ice cream starting to slide down his tongue back over the cornet.

A noise kicked David, a low drawn out note like speaker feedback, growling, louder and louder. It clogged his senses and he had to blink to remain focused, trying to close the gap and keep his footing at the same time. The sound reverberated through his head, twisting in a corkscrew. Then it stopped, along with a few seconds of reality. One moment he had been grimacing against the pain, Eddy close to the edge, the next the calm sea had simply closed over his son's head. No splash, no in between movement. Eddy had simply entered the water without causing a disturbance. David looked in horror as his son's small body receded into the depths; his arms tilted slightly away from his body and his hair pulled away from his head as though caught by a breeze.

A blast of sheer terror engulfed him; this panic, an accelerant to the fire already burning through his limbs.

Other people were moving now to help, but David was faster.

By the time David registered that the weight in his hands was from a broken sign, he was following it in a sharp arc into the water. He knew that without the weight he would have to fight to descend, and that this way he could keep his strength for the return journey.

There was a splash as someone else hit the waves a fraction of a second before he did. David was consumed by coldness. Water forced the air out of his ears, popping and cracking and pulling bubbles from his hair. At first he couldn't see anything, other than white spume, but felt the proximity of someone kicking close to him, clawing downward.

Then sound wasn't carried to him anymore. Had buoyancy fought the other swimmers back? He could imagine the surface choppy with limbs and bodies, but that couldn't explain the stillness that he felt above. David was dragged down, although he could feel the resistance pushing against him as though the sea wanted to eject him from its watery domain. The talisman of steel was stronger. Eddy should have been close, but David couldn't see his son. The blue murk stretched into blackness. Eddy should have been to his right and below. How far right depended upon how far the currents had moved him.

Worryingly, he couldn't see any of the supporting structure that he had been walking on. No pilings, rock faces, or even a sandy gradient. It was as though he had been dropped off into the middle of the ocean, far from the bright dappled surface. A horrible, impossible, thought formed. What if he was out to sea? Then suddenly, out of the gloom below, Eddy appeared as a motionless shape. He'd lost all contrast, aside from the faint smudge of colour from his shorts, appearing as a black and white phantom.

David's temples started to throb, his chest constricted. Physical pain started to wrack through his body, but he blocked it out, instead concentrating on his son who was getting closer and closer. His heartbeat was so pronounced that each contraction caused his arteries to beat in time. The air in his lungs had expanded, painfully stabbing against the inside of ribs as though he had inhaled a swarm of bees. Soon, he would have to exhale.

The low temperature might have shocked Eddy's body into a diving reflex. In some cases, young children had been resuscitated from up to forty-five minutes after drowning. The tragedy was the degree of impairment. If Eddy didn't drown, and his heartbeat had slowed dramatically, there was still a chance that he might come out of this without brain damage.

David exhaled slowly, knowing that once the last of his breath left his lungs, he would be well past the halfway point. The tendons in his arms were stretched to their limits, flesh white with pressure where he gripped the weight. Still he wouldn't let go. Not without his son.

And then he had no choice. David fell past Eddy. A strong upsurge reversed their positions. The makeshift diving weight spun away into the abyss, and David looked up.

They were not alone. A shadow outline of a ship's hull, only more rounded, was above them. A circle of light illuminated the surrounding waters, in comparison the sunlight above merely tinged the false dusk that had surrounded them. It wasn't a light source itself, rather an opening into whatever craft was above them.

Arms flailing, legs kicking like they had never kicked before, David reached out.

His fingers touched Eddy's smooth leg, before his son was drawn away from him, into the light.

David saw droplets slide from his son's now moving limbs, falling onto the surface, causing concentric circles to ripple across the aperture, saw Eddy's shimmering outline lean forwards, hair sliding to one side as he moved to help him. Eddy's fingers broke the surface tension, wavering above.

Desperate for contact, he let the last of the air out of his lungs, and lunged, but at the last moment he was buffeted away by a downward swell.

There was something behind Eddy, distorted grey and shapeless, by the refracted light. Something had him, was holding him back.

Then the opening vanished.

Immense pain exploded with a sharp crunch that was felt rather than heard, as half his outstretched hand was sheared away. David was knocked back, sent end over end by a powerful jet of water.

The shadow, and his son vanished.

He was hanging in empty space trapped within a band of twilight where light and dark coexisted, with his severed hand streaming a black cloud into the water. The freezing, crushing weight of the entire ocean was insignificant to the void that filled him. No air, far below the surface, all he could think about was Eddy.

Gone. Taken.

He was entirely alone.

Then, against his will, David took a breath.

David's life had a smaller footprint than before; noises from his house were muted, hushed and sombre as though the building had gone into mourning. People had rallied around at first, lent him sympathy, which they eventually took back when he made no sign of letting go. They didn't understand. Some even thought that he'd invented the story, some kind of defence mechanism to deny his responsibility. They might have nodded and smiled, but their eyes said, 'you're alive, your son is not.'

The doctor told him that he was he was lucky, the only damage from asphyxia had been to his lungs, and if he remained shackled to a portable oxygen bottle, he could maintain a relatively normal life.

And then there were the hallucinations.

Just when he thought that he was getting better. Something would happen. He'd hear Eddy's voice in the night, calling out for a drink; or a hug; or giggling in the hallway, and that would upset him again. One night he awoke to find himself carrying a glass of water into Eddy's deserted bedroom, only waking by catching his injured hand on the door trying to work the handle. David sank down on the child sized bed and placed the glass on the bedside table amongst the others. He realised that the house was nothing more than a lifeless shell. He had turned a sanctuary into a mausoleum. A family could put the rooms to better use, imprint their own memories upon the bricks and plaster, cover over the posters and stickers that he and Eddy had put there, the ones that he couldn't look at anymore.

Life continued or rather, those to whom he owed money to, tried to intrude. They would phone at first, then after a while send letters. Those brown envelopes remained unopened where they landed on the doormat. Later the phone stopped ringing, and later still, confused by its absence, David lifted the receiver and was unable to get a dial tone.

David sold the house and rented an apartment by the coast. For a while the visions became worse, then, they got better. Nightmares followed through into his waking world, though not all were unwelcome. He saw Eddy, older and tanned, looking for his bucket, the red one that they had left at the beach that day, but David didn't know where it went. In another, he was observing Eddy move through white corridors, crying, calling for him, but those weren't the worst. By far the most disturbing were the ones where David himself wandered through the corridors, sure his son was just in the next room, or the next... or the next.

At the evening's arrival David makes his way to the shore, as he has for the past year, watching the sun set across the black ocean, hoping, praying to see the silhouette of a small boy running along the sands.

As he listens to the gentle sound of the waves lapping against the stones, he wonders.

Wonders that if he jumped in, what he would find there. Wonders if Eddy is waiting for him, ready to pluck him from the depths into a halo of light, or if the light will be last thing his oxygen deprived brain decodes, stretching out into oblivion.

He knows that when the pain gets too much, he will try.

A LONG WAY HOME

The weather report said minus forty. It was just a number too abstract in my mind to mean anything. Two digits with a little dash in front. What did it mean? Forty was warm, so was that the flip side? The absence of warmth?

How bad could it be? Cold is cold. I'd never been out in temperatures so low - perhaps in my ignorance it would be my last. I'd read about these exact same situations in the papers, or caught them on the news, of people heading out into freak weather conditions, made more tragic by the fact that they froze to death not far from their own doorstep.

Don't go out. That was the warning: don't go out. It had sounded strange to my ears, I'd expected the 'unless necessary,' to follow, the common sense warning applied for those who had none. Again, it was the first time that a weather anchor had used an imperative. She looked into the camera, shrugged as though embarrassed and then the screen cut to the mid-range forecast. Winter usually meant a couple of degrees below and manageable snowfall, but times were changing. I'd always assumed that global warming meant that things would be getting warmer, anything but this. Snow drifts ten feet deep, undulating over the landscape in dunes.

The snap blizzard conditions had caught the country off guard. I shook my head, but what would you expect from a nation of people who plant trees alongside rail tracks to protect the sensibilities of their neighbours, but couldn't handle leaves on the tracks when they fell. We might only have one word for snow, but plenty to describe those who lack common sense.

I had no choice. Our daughter was dying, burning up with a fever, skin cracking and blistering. Her delicate fingers purple, with blackening nail beds.

There was no alternative. We couldn't move her. If it wasn't me, then it would be Ellie, my wife, who would go, and she'd already threatened to once already. No sane person would venture out in weather like this. We both knew that and I prepared for my journey in silence.

Ellie tracked down a doctor online, managed to show them our stricken child using a web cam in order to get a remote diagnosis.

Telephones were down, power was too, but miraculously I'd managed to use a laptop to hop across shared Wi-Fi connections, to bypass frozen streets and contact a chemist who stocked the medication that would save Raylee's life. The only problem was that it was four miles away.

We were in the same boat with her last year, waiting for a transplant donor, but she pulled through. I was on first name terms with the spectre of hopelessness. Not this time. It was within my power to help.

Ellie clung to my arm, "Give it another hour, the fever might break."

I wasn't sure who she was trying to convince, but the storm had passed leaving a fresh blanket of glistening snow. Four miles, it wasn't that far. Normally I could have jogged there and back in an hour. Minus forty, okay, if it slowed me down a little. A mile an hour? I could still get back in a couple of hours. Hell, I would crawl if need be.

I peered out of the curtains, pulling them to one side, but couldn't see anything but thick frost on the glass. There were chinks and cracks running through the pane, where the surround had contracted.

Ellie reluctantly helped me climb into my outdoors

gear, I felt like an astronaut suiting up. Before the laptop battery died, I'd messaged the guy to let them know that I was on my way, and use the last of the laptop battery to check the weather one more time.

Another storm due in four hours. I thought to myself there was no way that I'd need that long.

I'd taken as many precautions as I could. Five layers of clothing; two coats; three pairs of gloves including a pair of Ellie's pink woollen ones; a scarf that I'd wrap around my face, and a pair of swimming goggles. I left my hood down until the last moment. Once up it would restrict my vision to that of looking through a fist sized tunnel.

There was a thermos flask full of scalding coffee and hot water bottles strapped to the inside of my coat.

No one else would be able to collect the medicine, and they sure as hell wouldn't deliver.

Don't go out, remember?

But without the medicine Raylee would die.

I took a deep breath, then slipped the scarf over my mouth.

The front door opened to a solid wall. I stared at the blueness, the sheer solidity, at the shapes and shadows trapped within. Light shimmered through, giving it the appearance of a deep sea aquarium, and us observing from beneath the waves.

"I think," I said. "I think, I can see our car." In the distance, suspended in curlicues of smoked white swirls was the family car.

"It's so clear!" Ellie said.

"All the air's been squashed out; it's been compacted down."

I felt the force of the cold explore the surfaces I presented, running its curious fingers over my armour, nipping and pulling at the joints in the layers. Ellie's face was red raw, slapped by the change. I closed the door. For a moment I feared that the ice had encroached that single millimetre forward, putting its immense shoulder against the wooden frame to keep it open, but the lock clicked shut.

When the door closed, the cowardly heat rushed to reclaim the void. Safe within the folds of my pockets, I could feel the flask burning my hip and the water bottles toasting my chest.

Not to be deterred, I kissed Raylee goodbye.

I ended up sliding out of the bathroom window. It was the only portal that I could open that was large enough to climb through.

My gloves stuck to the snow, tearing and popping, leaving black threaded finger prints. A drift had swallowed the front of the house, leaving a gentle slope to the first floor windows.

Once down, I adjusted the scarf over my mouth, my exposed skin burning and cracking. Even breathing through the scarf my lungs seared as if I was inhaling fire. I stumbled, blinking rapidly, startled by the sheer immediacy of the cold's attack. Cobwebs encroached at the corners of goggles and they stuck to my face. I forced the air through my teeth, through the woven material over my mouth. Wheezing in and out, I stood for a moment, wondering what it sounded like.

Ellie raised her hand once, behind the now closed window, and I was off.

The ground beneath my feet seemed to begrudge my presence, snapping and biting as I put one foot in front of the other.

Around me the buildings were all uniform, frosted decorations. Street lights and sign posts had become small obstacles to step over. A set of traffic lights on the corner flooded their surroundings with a deep red light, the amber and green buried beneath the ice.

I took a moment to start the stopwatch that Ellie had

taped to the outside of my jacket. While the deepest part of the snow had been crushed solid by the weight pressed down upon it, the upper layer was as thin as talc.

A single flake fell from the bright sky; I heard it softly pat against my hood.

The surrounding landscape was dead or dying. Nothing stirred. Even my own house looked deserted, Ellie and Raylee huddled in the living room that had become a subterranean lair, cowering by candlelight.

Telegraph poles had been torn down, betrayed by wires coated in layer upon layer of ice. Streetlights had bowed below the weight or sheared off at the base and were caught in a solid river of debris.

It wasn't long before I realised that only the desperate and demented were out.

At a junction, I saw a thick overcoat discarded next to a shop awning. Further on, other items of clothes. It ended at two naked frozen bodies. I'd heard that hypothermia could make you do that. When your core reaches a certain temperature, you feel as though you're actually getting warmer. Someone could be freezing to death, but feel as though they were baking, walking through a desert. I remembered this, because I always liked the term it was given: paradoxical undressing.

The sun shone through a break in the clouds, fizzing where its rays touched, adding to the chorus of white noise. More flakes fell.

The further into the city I went, the more sheltered from the wind it became. Metal hulls dotted along the highway were buried like sunken wrecks with aerials poking out of the drifts. There were scarves tied to some. I stopped, banged on the roof of one, and scraped away the ice to see the cyanotic occupants inside, their eyes crystallised and staring.

That's when it really dawned on me: this is how the world ends.

Above, thick clouds, pregnant with more death,

clogged the sunlight once more.

The owner of the pharmacy had been watching out for me. I would have walked by if he hadn't stepped in my way. Made huge by the volume of clothes he wore, he took my elbow and dragged me inside.

"This will be the death of me," he said. The hallway wasn't much warmer than outside, only there was no wind. Wooden panels, tortured by the wintry grip wept amber and resin. He saw me looking and said, "This end of the world business sure does make a mess doesn't it?"

"Really do appreciate this," I said.

"Ayup."

"How much do I owe you?"

He laughed. The only warm thing in the room.

"Anyone who can walk more than ten yards in that deserves it. I'll pray for you, for yours."

I followed him to the shop floor. Like the rest of the building, the cold had claimed most of the rooms. Bottles had become like candles, disgorging multi-hued icicles. Shampoo waterfalls, in a creamy purple and red display adorned one wall. I could smell smoke and hear the crackle of a fire. They were burning furniture to keep warm, pulled up floorboards and cabinet doors rested against the hearth. I looked at his bright red face.

"You checking for carbon monoxide?" I asked.

He nodded.

"Damned if you don't, damned if you do."

"Bit of Hobson's, well ventilated means being cold. I'm not sure how much longer I want to be cold, if you follow my meaning. Only been keeping a window open this long so that there would be someone here when you arrived."

"I really appreciate it."

The heat was nearly unbearable after being outside for so long. The warmer air felt like red hot needles poking into my limbs as I stood. I felt sweat trickle down my back. I felt light headed, too; maybe from the amount of monoxide in the air.

"May you find peace," the pharmacist said, holding out a bag.

There was more than just the medicine in there. I took it.

"Thanks."

"The one that you want is the blue bottle, label on the top. I've filled it with a few other things that you might need, not now, but later, if there is a later."

"Will it be okay carried like this?"

The pharmacist thought for a moment, "Yeah, the liquids have plenty of expansion room to freeze. Just make sure that you thaw them thoroughly before you use them. You should inject every four hours. There's some pills and powders. Bandages and plasters for your frostbite."

"Frostbite?"

"End of your nose is turning, ears as well."

I touched the side of my head and it was like shooting my head with a stapler.

"Be careful. The weather's taking a turn for the worse. Before we lost signal, they were saying that a deep freeze is coming. Minus fifty or sixty."

I nodded.

My watch said that the first four miles had taken two hours.

"Any word from Ellie?"

"No. As I said, signal dropped out after we got your request. Not heard anything from anyone else."

"Thanks, again."

He shrugged, "Anytime."

I thought that I'd never been so cold.

Then the storm hit.

Less than five minutes and I couldn't think. My head crushed in a burning vice and the pain in my ears so bad they were on fire. I felt sick, guilty for wanting to stop, but in so much pain that I couldn't move. I dropped my gaze, ducked in to the edge of the street to try and get a little shelter from the buildings there. Each step was ponderous, taking an eternity to complete. The white powder I'd waded through on the way was now blasting through the air, stinging and choking.

The cold was shearing away my extremities.

If I could get out of the wind, shelter awhile and let the worst pass, I could continue. Liquid thoughts, soothing thoughts, probably the same that went through the minds of those who made it no further. Last thoughts, considered by people only found in the spring when the snows had melted.

No it wouldn't take me the same way.

I had to get back to Ellie, for Raylee's sake.

It couldn't claim me if I kept moving. I couldn't feel my limbs, and my trousers cracking. The air was heavy, like walking through cement.

Ice clad. Slowing, fighting inertia, getting worse and worse. I had to pull the goggles from my face, taking a layer of skin away with them and instantly my eyelashes froze. Ice expanded on my eyelids, their sharp prongs digging into my eyes, scratching my cornea when I blinked.

I glanced at my watch to see that each second took an age to roll over. Staring, I became sure that I could count to five before the next increment rolled over.

My legs pushed against the snow, wading through the fresh fall, after a while I could no longer follow the trail that I'd made on the way in and forged a new path.

My scarf was pulled loose by the wind, jerking away from my face and slashing back, slicing into my cheek, cutting and scalding at the same time.

Ghosts of the land rose up, shadows of figures who weren't there stalked the edge of my vision. Whenever I looked, the shape dissolved into the blizzard, sending dagger-like shards at me.

The storm was alive. Some hulking beast just out of sight, waiting, watching me. I could feel it lurking, wanting me to stop.

Ahead stooped a dark, looming figure, a fifteen-foot-tall, crooked street lamp, the metal hood cracked and chewed. My heart missed a beat, then another, becoming arrhythmic. My limbs refused to move, resisting my insistent commands. Arms falling to my side, my shoulders drooped. Stop and die from exposure, or continue into the awaiting maw of the beast.

But I couldn't stop.

I had to go on.

Bowing my head, I took another step forward, taunting the creature. I expected to feel its talons tear through my clothes, to rend the flesh from my back but it didn't.

The spirit of the storm raged against me, throwing more darkness and swirling flurries of snow. It wasn't going to end this way. I'd come so far. It couldn't end this way.

I railed against the fury of the storm, using it to feed my desire to get home.

The storm kept pace. Ahead the street brightened, but as soon as I arrived at the point where I had perceived the light to be, it grew dark and windswept, as though I was the thunderhead itself.

I suddenly recognised where I was.

It was my street.

Our house was no more than fifty feet away. I looked at my watch, rubbing the face to reveal the time. Seven hours fifty. I'd walked eight miles and taken nearly a full day. But I was back!

Then I noticed that the front door was visible, the ground beneath my feet wasn't icebound, but speckled with a light dusting. The power too was fixed. Previously fallen posts, righted and correct.

What was going on?

A light was on inside. I pulled the gloves from my fingers as I raced to the door.

I'd not taken a key with me, so I tried the handle. It was locked.

I banged on the familiar panel with the heel of my palm.

There was movement from within, behind the glass window, unhurried.

I saw a shape move, stoop, then heard the key scrape in the lock.

Ellie opened the door, her eyes wide with fright.

I took a step back, shocked at her expression. "Oh god, am I too late? Is Raylee okay? Tell me?"

Her frame crumpled against the frame. "Is… is it really you?"

I pulled open the bag, my black fingers numb, their grip uncertain at first, then I held the medicine out to her.

"I've got it, it's here! Am I too late?"

She stared at me and didn't answer for a long time. When she did, it chilled me more than the elements had.

"But you left three years ago," she said standing on the doorstep. Pulling her cardigan tighter about her frame. "Raylee's dead. She died."

I faltered. Ellie was the same, but the more I looked, the more I saw the changes. Wrinkles that weren't there when I left this morning, and her eyes reflected a sadness that didn't belong.

What was happening?

I retracted my hand. No, this was a phantom, a manifestation of the weather to destroy my hope, make me give up. My hands closed over the bottle, and I felt frost spread over the glass.

The digits on the watch still moved, eight hours had elapsed. That's all I'd been, eight hours. But, what was she saying? Three years?

I could feel the heat pulsating behind the doors like poison, and I knew that I was a world away from where she was now. Ellie stepped to one side, so that I could see beyond her into our hallway, where my paintings still hung.

"Come in," she said reluctantly.

A voice from behind asked, "Who is it? Shut the door love, it's cold."

I laughed. Why not. If I could imagine my wife three years from now, I could also imagine that she'd moved on. Three years was long enough to get over her dead husband and child. That would explain the glimmer of sadness. Or rather, that's what the spirit of winter wanted me to believe. Crush the hope from my soul, take away all reason for living.

I'd gone mad. Time was ticking, snow swirled about my head and shoulders and Ellie frowned her face scoured raw, until at last she had to step back.

My mind fractured, a cold splinter rejecting and accepting what was before me.

Receding from the doorway, I turned away

I howled. A bestial call with all the fury of the storm. There was still time. I had to shut it all out, forget everything. I checked the watch, seeing the digits tick on.

My wife and daughter were out there, somewhere, and I'd find them.

All I had to do was keep walking. Keep walking home.

Where I walked, the fury of the storm followed.

THE OTHER SIDE

Drunk, weaving my way along an unfamiliar corridor, clutching what is either the last of a single digit count of beers, or first in double figures. The lights kaleidoscope different hues from recessed fittings and with each blink, revellers strobe into open spaces like a Ray Harryhausen picture. Litter and empty beer bottles congregate in the corners, swept there by passing feet.

There are doors on either side that would normally be closed, exposing single bed dorms which are part of the faculty's halls of residence. Austere and basic, the confined space make the party even more conspicuous. Like raging fire, it has spilled into the communal corridors demanding attention. There's an added air of nervous excitement on top of the merriment, as everyone knows it could be stopped at any time. The lift arriving invokes a Pavlovian response in those standing too close: bottles jerk behind backs and faces twitch with shocked grimaces.

Bobbing along with the current of people I peer into their faces, hoping to find someone I recognise. I don't want to spend the night haunting the corridor trying to find some familiar group to attach myself to. The night too young to go home, but too late to leave to find another venue.

And I needed another piss even though I'd just been.

I took another long gulp of beer, feeling the liquid sink just below my throat and I closed my eyes, fighting the sensation of the froth lapping against my tonsils. One thing for sure, I'd be getting value for money the next time

I did pay a visit it.

"Hey!"

I jumped, turning to the source of the noise. "Hey!" a woman's voice shouted.

She was standing close, touching my elbow to anchor herself in place. Her hair was a radiant rainbow, tied in bunches that floated above paint splattered dungarees. She wore a rope belt that cinched her waist and dangling streamers that whispering in time to the music.

My eyes closed again fighting the alcohol, "Yeah?" I slurred.

"Could you help me?"

I figured that I was pretty much incapable of anything unless she wanted a doorstop. That I could manage. Maybe I should go home. If I stayed I'd likely make a mess. It wouldn't be the first time, and God forbid, wouldn't be the last.

"Wadda you want?" I hated myself. I sounded rude and the alcohol fumes on my breath were staring to make my eyes sting.

"We need someone to sit in a circle, would you join us?"

Her request didn't sound too much of an ask, "Yeah, why not?"

"Follow me," she said, gently leading me by my elbow inside the room.

She let go of my arm once she'd positioned me at the edge of a small circle of people. The room looked like cheap hotel room, chipboard furniture next to an emaciated wardrobe and a bed that was no more than a mattress forced into a sunken frame. The walls had been personalised by blotting out the battleship grey paint with colourful posters: an eclectic mishmash of occult and fantasy symbols, and a large, almost beatific, Cthulhu waiting for a bus behind his painfully thin creator H.P. Lovecraft.

The bad news was that there was no sign of anyone

familiar, but the good news was that my bladder hadn't given out yet. Besides, I couldn't possibly need to go so soon. Ignoring the shooting pains, I hoped it would go away.

I looked at her expectant face, yeah - where was the harm in staying? After all, first year at uni, it was supposed to be about making friends, and what were strangers but friends I've yet to meet.

"So what now?" I asked.

"For the moment, we're just having a chat, my name is Chaucer, this is Anna..." and a quick barrage of names followed. Faces nodded in my direction, but they seemed distant. Or maybe I was the obnoxious drunk that had simply been dragged to make up the numbers, and they were humouring me.

My knees popped as I crouched down and turned to Anna.

"I'm Bryan," I said. I couldn't place what course I was on, something technical, but I couldn't form the title in my head. Computing in something. Or Business and? How embarrassing. There was a skinny fella to my right, but I couldn't remember his name and didn't want to ask. Instead, I turned away from him. He probably remembered his course title. Anna was probably his girlfriend. Ah well.

I could hear Chaucer talking to a couple of people on the other side, so I was half listening.

"I have a hole in my head," Chaucer was saying.

"What's that like?" Someone asked.

In my mind the words passed through a filter, and I started to hum 'Head like a hole.' It took a couple of seconds for that to equate to the funny looks that people were giving me. Obviously not Reznor fans.

"...Most of the time it's like looking into a dark well."

"Most of the time?" I asked.

"Occasionally someone or something comes through?"

I raised my eyebrows. This was getting a little too

kooky for my liking. Anna seemed nice though, I decided that I'd stick it out for a couple more minutes, then use the toilet break as a get out of jail free card.

"Like tonight?" The group exchanged glances.

A cold chill started spreading across my thighs. For a split second, I thought I'd wet myself. When I looked, the guy next to me was pouring beer onto my crotch.

"Easy with the sharing, pal! I've already got plenty!"

He jolted away, raining beer on the people to his right. He flung himself backwards with such force that he was up against the end of the bed, trying to work his way into the frame with his shoulders. "S-s-s-orry dude."

My fingers dragged across the top of the spill, flicking droplets to the floor. It would dry, eventually. State I was in I didn't really care too much anyway, not enough to get into a fight over, besides, I'd probably do worse myself before the evening was out.

I could really feel the room spin and shutting out the world didn't make it feel any better.

Anna asked quietly, "So how are you finding it?"

I felt a hand on my arm; the breath of a whisper on my cheek. It felt good. Above the thrum of the bass coming through the floor and the hubbub of conversations in different rooms, I felt at ease. I no longer wanted had to get home. I was in a drink fuelled sanctuary.

I'd not really had chance to talk to anyone else about starting university. My older brother left school at fifteen for the army, he was twenty now, but his interests extended no further than what he could hold in his hands, be it money, women, or guns.

I hiccupped.

Budweiser took away my inhibitions, and I found myself saying "Completely overwhelming."

It was.

When I'd arrived I'd not expected anywhere near the workload. Every lecturer dished out months of homework. At the end of the first day, I had at least six months' worth of work to get through. "I must admit, after the first week, I was ready to pack it in. How can anyone deal with that sort of change? It wasn't what I expected — but everything seems to be settling down nicely." I rolled my head in her direction, she was staring with rapt attention. I didn't have anything else to say, but because no one else was talking, I felt I had to continue, "It helps not to take things too seriously, and I get out to see my friends once in a while," I raised my bottle, "and have a beer."

I shifted uneasily. The rest were listening intently. Christ, what was it with these people?

After a while they returned to talking amongst themselves.

"This is boring," I said. I really needed to pay a visit, so I started to stand.

"Please stay, we're only just starting," Chaucer said.

"Starting? No thanks, I gotta go. People to see."

I hoisted myself to my feet and the room swayed me out of the door into the corridor.

A wave of nausea carried bile to the back of my throat and I coughed in the hallway. Putting a hand out against the wall to steady myself. The beer tide was definitely coming in.

A moment later, the lights went out. The hallway became a black void. Not even the sound of stereos continued. Everything stopped.

I couldn't see. The doors sprang shut as soon as the power went, the echo of the automatic fasteners clicking in my ears. Disoriented, I turned, trying to find my way back to the party. The room should have been close.

Maybe I'd walked past? So I turned, didn't recognise anything so turned again, then lost track of which way I had been walking down in the first place. After a few moments of searching, finally I could see it: the glimmer of candle light creeping from beneath a door.

A bright light spread from behind ruining my night vision. I turned. A guy stepped out with a flashlight, shining it in my face. It could have been spilly-beard, but I wasn't sure.

"You okay?" he asked. He didn't sound like the guy who'd poured beer over me.

"Yeah, yeah," I waved the bottle at him. "Just finding my friends."

"Power cut," he said, stating the obvious.

No shit Sherlock.

He closed the door behind him, and once again the corridor was in darkness. I waited for my eyes to adjust. After a moment, I could make out the crack of light from halfway down the corridor.

"Hello," I called. "Hello? Anna? Chaucer?"

Candlelight flickered from a door and I could make out movement in the room. Laughter? Talking as well? I stepped forward and my forehead cracked against glass. Fireworks went off in my temple, and sparks shot down my optic nerves like stars into a black hole. It was a door, a fire door, that was all. I laughed. It must have closed with the others. My fingers spider walked across the surface trying to find a handle.

Sagging against the cold surface, I could see the light on the other side. The party was continuing halfway down the corridor, in that room beyond. I could make out shadows moving.

I must have lost my bearings in the darkness.

The only way is through.

The door shifted slightly against my weight.

I took a step back, and launched myself forward, wanting to give it a tap with my shoulder.

Glass shattered. I bashed my head on the frame on my way through, cursing as I fell. I put my hands out, expecting to come to an abrupt stop on the other side, but there was no floor, only empty air and stars.

I fell end over end.

Just as I had twenty years before.

Dear Mark,

You said that going to university would be the best thing for me. You were right, it's only taken me five years to realise.

The first week into term and I've already met this awesome girl on my course. She's into channelling and spiritualism. I know what you think, but this isn't like that. It probably sounds so convenient coming from me, but I tell you, the hardest lie to disprove is the truth. I'm not trying to convince you, so you're going to have to trust me on this one. I wish there was some way to share the experience, other than this letter, but you weren't there. I can already hear your voice in my head, muttering about group hysteria, or drug induced hallucinations. Yeah, yeah big bro, it wasn't that kind of party.

Her name was Chaucer. I'm not sure if it was her forename or surname but she carried it well. Turns out she has a room in the dorm on the university campus. The one where a student killed himself back in 1999. She brought him back in front of six witnesses. She told us to form a circle and talk about anything; to always to use the present tense and not say anything about suicide.

Mad really. After I'd spent all those years looking for, I don't know, help? Support? That I find it when it was most unexpected.

I didn't believe her at first. I know what you're thinking, if I didn't take her seriously, then why was I there? Simple, I never lost hope, not like you. I didn't give up, not once.

Halfway through the evening Chaucer stood and went to the door. When she opened it there was no one there. She talked to herself on the threshold for a couple of seconds and then returned to her place in the circle. Only there was something clinging to her arm, something or someone unseen.

She gestured to the floor and I saw her posture change

as though a weight had fallen from her. I could feel a presence next to me. I couldn't see anything, but it felt right. Chaucer said to talk about something, so I turned to this empty space and introduced myself. His voice came from nowhere. He said his name was Bryan. I was talking to a dead guy! Ha. I've already thought of a few jokes about that, so you can tell me yours when I see you.

The short of it is that I had a conversation with someone on the other side! Jimmy, one of the other guys was being a dick. He poured beer on the floor next to me, but it didn't land on the carpet. Not straight away. It pooled in mid-air for a second, before being splashed across the room!

I wasn't scared.

I asked him what the afterlife was like.

He said that it was overwhelming. Completely, and not what he expected, but he was figuring it out as he went. He said that he's not alone, that he gets to see his friends once in a while, how cool is that?

That's good.

Anyway, that was the reason that I was getting in touch. It's your anniversary this week. I've got the flowers for your grave.

I bought myself a new knife at the weekend. This time I said it was for paper. It has surgical steel blades. When I'm cutting, I'm imagining that it's the veins in my arms. Sounds strange doesn't it, but taking up a hobby has helped.

I miss you.

I really do.

I've one last project to complete before I come over.

If Bryan's right, then I'll see you soon, if I'm mistaken, it doesn't matter. It's been ten years and everything ends, eventually. Even pain.

Your loving sister,
Anna.

THE FALL

This high up, the wind stings his face, pinching his tear streaked cheeks. From below, the midnight noise from the streets are muted and distorted. The cold makes him feel alive.

Ironic really.

With shaking hands, he removes his music player. The sleek glass display, although like ice, responds quickly to his numb fingers as they swipe backwards and forwards.

The track he selects is a favourite. One that until now has kept even his blackest thoughts at bay.

Not thinking, just listening. His feet move in small unconscious circles as he dangles them over the edge. His nose tickles from the cold, the temperature taking the edge off the aroma. There's a faint tang of stale urine clinging to the concrete, mixed with exhaust fumes and rain.

He's out of the way, up on the highest level of the car park, over the other side of the solid barrier. No one can see him from this level, maybe if they were close enough to the edge on the level below, then they might be able to look up and see the soles of his shoes, but there's no one around.

He jams his hands back into his pockets and closes his eyes.

As the music rises, he smiles to himself.

If only he could stretch this moment to infinity, he would.

Everything has to come to an end.

Could he go through with it?

It would be so easy to pull his legs back and climb back over the railing. He could walk down the exit ramp and keep going. No one would ever be the wiser.

Who was he kidding?

He couldn't go home. That route forever closed.

The only reason the phone in his pocket is silent, is because he's turned it off. It nestles against his ribs, close to the pair that she'd fractured last time he was late.

Remembering this made him resolute. It wasn't a cry for help. No one would listen. No one cared. Running away now would only delay the inevitable.

A shiver runs through his back and he twitches, feeling the seams of his jeans catch on the cement that he's perched upon.

Some decisions can't be undone. Believing so, is a flight of fancy, and nothing more.

The track ends.

He closes his eyes and tips forward.

A moment of nausea follows as his stomach rotates weightlessly as he tips end over end. Vertigo, he thinks, but can't be that because he actually is spinning. In the silence between tracks, he welcomes death.

Then it all goes wrong.

He had considered that there might be a moment of hurt. Hitting the ground from this height would split him open like an egg. He'd researched this means of suicide before. Bodies bounce. Not much, but they do. From this height the impact would liquefy his organs. There might be a sudden firework going off in his head as his synapses shorted, but it would be over like a shot. Or so he hoped.

For a moment, he is the physical embodiment of agony. A series of blinding impacts go off in quick succession. Head, back, then his shoulder. He spirals. His chest crushes into itself. Instinctively he tries to move his hands to reach the pain, but they are deep within the folds of his coat, and something immobile has passed between his arm and his chest. Centrifugal forces grip harder, rattling him around like a rag doll on a spinning top. His hand trapped in his coat forms a loop, which is forced wider and wider by an immobile object, larger than his arm can stretch. The pressure at his shoulder increases, burning, tearing.

He passes out as his body comes apart.

For a long time he wants to die.

For a longer time, he thinks he will. Unable to communicate, a prisoner within his own body, he tries to make something move, anything move so that he can tap out a message. Never having learnt Morse code, he prays that if he holds his breath long enough they realise that he doesn't want to go on, but he can't, he doesn't have control over his muscles enough even to do that.

What's worse, lying in this sharp world, is knowing that it won't end.

Days pass.

Weeks pass.

He doesn't know how long he's been like this.

Then something changes, a realisation that he can't die. Even if he wanted to. Something is keeping him alive.

Dreams come and go, and he's lucid for longer periods.

He remembers falling.

Bright lights hover above his head. Not that he can open his eyes, just gain a sense of redness through eyelids that won't open.

Sounds, smells - disinfectant, chlorine, blood. Darkness.

Out of the darkness, his existence is floating above a pit of needles. Sometimes he is lowered into it, experiencing the agony. Over time, he realises that it's medication that keeps him suspended.

He grows use to the steady drip, drip, of morphine into a bag, and the icy embrace it brings.

Time has no meaning. Not the monotonous chirp of the machines that keep him alive, or the number of times that the door to his room opens. Trapped within his flesh prison, he only gets an impression of those that attend him, ghosts outside of his senses.

Eventually, even this phantoms become individuals.

He recognises their signature sounds; the squeak of the plimsolls the anaesthetist wears, the clunk and scrape of the janitor's mop and bucket.

This is what his life has been pared down to. So simple that he can begin to let go, forget all the suffering and hate. All he has to do is get better.

The door opens.

There are no footsteps.

If it had been a nurse, doctor, they would have been close by now. Flitting like fireflies to the equipment around him, or to one of the many injection points to administer pain relief or antibiotics.

He fights against the paralysis that holds him to the bed, managing to move an inch, but nothing more.

The sinking sensation continues. It's the hitch of breath he recognises, the intake before the flow of venom.

"I know that you're awake," she hisses. This is the voice of his tormentor. Not the woman he married, but who she turned into. Devolved, she became more and more feral the longer they stayed together.

"The doctor tells me that you can hear. I know you're awake."

There is nothing else he can do. He is the absolute definition of a captive audience.

"You really made a mess of yourself. They brought parts of you back in a bucket." She snorts, "Just in case they could reattach anything."

He remembers his right arm. Caught and torn. Disarticulated.

Sensing she is close, he can feel the blankets on his body being lifted, fingers drumming on the protective body cast that entombs his remains.

She is silent for a second. "You couldn't have got rid of that while you were at it."

There's a sigh. "I always knew that I had more balls that you."

He wishes to die all again. Whatever is keeping him alive would pack up, or he could stop his beating heart just by thinking it.

"No way is your medical going to cover this. What the fuck am I going to do? I'm not getting a job to pay for your fucking treatment."

There's a dragging sensation. Thankfully he's too full of morphine to feel the pain that follows, but he can hear a pop and splash as a catheter is removed.

"You better hope you fucking die."

There's a squeak and a draught washes over him from a newly opened window.

A lighter rasps a few times. He smells burning paraffin, catches the rank whiff of tobacco. He hears a glottal pop close to his face, then smoke, in a long stream blows over his mouth.

It bites the back of his throat like a viper and his chest heaves. His inside feels full of broken glass. Wracking coughs cause him to spasm like a severed worm, writhing against his shell.

She drops the burning cigarette down the opening of his neck cast.

"You think how you're going to pay for all this."

The door opens. "Is everything alright in here?"

Her voice becomes sweetness and light. "Just giving my husband some encouragement. His wife's voice swirls around like the witch around Dorothy from Oz. There's no place like home. No place... home. No home.

Then she's gone.

He weeps - as much as his injuries allow. This is hell. There is no escape, and it's not as though he can tell anyone about what happened.

"What the...!" A voice startles him. Rich and smooth, like the low notes on a piano. He can feel strong hands grip his shoulders, pull him back into position on the bed.

A needle grazes his arm.

"You got to be careful moving around, pulled out your drip."

He wants to scream it was her, not him. But he can't. No sound escapes.

"That's better," the voice says. "You're all hooked up."

He feels a hand on his shoulder. "Did you pull this out yourself, can you move?"

Nothing, his limbs are lead weights once more.

His tongue lies still.

"I'll be back with the doctor, check you out make sure that you haven't done yourself an injury."

But by the time they return, he's unconscious again.

"Oh my God. I am so sorry." This is the first time he has heard this particular voice. Male, young, emotive, but that's all he can glean.

A soft sigh. "Jesus. Where to begin... Okay, okay, I can do this." There's another pause. He can feel this newcomer pace backwards and forwards at the bottom of the hospital bed. The zip to the man's coat catches on the clipboard that he knows is tucked into the tray in the frame, just once.

"My name is Michael. I work for the company that looks after your insurance claim. Well, I'm an investigator, trying to make sure that it doesn't pay out if it doesn't have to. Sorry, I'm rambling..."

The life support machine wheezes, distracting the speaker momentarily.

"I know what you tried to do. I don't hold it against you, you know shit happens. Normally in similar circumstances, if we can prove that the individual tried to take their own life, then we're not at liberty to honour the policy.

"What we have here is a bit of a grey area. Most of the times people try, they end up in A&E and then go home, we're none the wiser - or they succeed, and the people that are left behind sort out the mess. A good deal of the time policies don't get cashed anyway, because the person who killed themselves often dealt with the paperwork, and in all the confusion, something as insignificant as assurance falls between the cracks.

"Unfortunately, you survived. If your intention was to kill yourself, you had a pretty good go at it. A foot to the left, or if you didn't have your hand in your pocket when you hit the flag pole, then perhaps you've have succeeded. In that case, you'd be... more fucked. I would have looked at the circumstances and closed your case since you breached the terms of the policy. Rightly so. No one parks on the second highest floor of a multi-story car park at three in the morning, climbs over a shoulder height wall, unless they have something serious in mind.

"But you survived, and this is where it gets complicated. Your wife is adamant that you spoke to her that night, saying that you'd dropped your keys onto the ledge, and were going to retrieve them. Why you'd phone her and tell her this, I have no idea. I can't prove otherwise, I contacted your mobile phone provider and they couldn't help me with any records. Fortunate glitch or something.

"Anyway I've done some digging.

"When I spoke to your wife, she seemed devastated, quite a vulnerable young woman." He clears his throat, "It just seemed too contrived. You know why you're still here? Your life support should have been turned off a couple of weeks ago. She wants to keep you alive - if it can be called that, while the insurance claim goes through. You're amassing a good deal of debt here. She's making a big gamble.

"She needs the pay out as much as you do.

"Hell, anyone who looks at your credit card transactions after you took the fall would get a similar impression. Only I can't do anything about it. Even with all the evidence, it's subjective. You know what she's like, you lived with her, I've seen the paperwork and I'm guessing, but I think I also have a good idea of what she's like.

"It took her ten weeks to come and visit. About the same time that the limits were being reached on two of your credit cards. She got a loan, in your name, which I can only assume that she's living off, because there's no other income I can see, and she's been hounding my office for a decision.

"You're still here because of her.

"I can't change your circumstances. While I believe that the system is being abused, it's not you that's doing it.

"If I tell the company what I think, then it doesn't stop. She's not going to let this go. I can foresee a huge legal fight around who picks up your bill and you end up getting pushed to whoever is the cheapest service provider. If you die, she gets a legitimate angle for suing us, and the emphasis shifts from what you did, to what we didn't do. It turns out that keeping you alive is going to be the cheapest option. But only we dictate the terms.

"I'm getting you transferred to a secure unit, she won't be able to trace you.

"Just get better. While you're like this, then there's always a chance that she can find a way to take advantage.

"Dying isn't an option.

"Everyone falls once in a while. Sometimes we can catch them before they hit the bottom. Sometimes they have to bounce a few times first.

"Don't give up."

He feels something that he's not felt in a long time. Hope.

ABOUT THE AUTHOR

You can find out more about John Winter, if you want to, on facebook:

https://www.facebook.com/InAColdDarkPlace

on twitter: @OldDarkWriter

or drop by his website
http://olddarkwriter.wixsite.com/johnwinter

Printed in Great Britain
by Amazon